SALIE.

By

Si Rosser

Schmall World Publishing

First published in Great Britain as an e-book by Schmall World
Publishing

Copyright © Simon Rosser 2017

SALIENT

By

Si Rosser

Also by the same author;

The A-Z of Global Warming

Tipping Point – Robert Spire 1

Impact Point – Robert Spire 2

Melt Zone – Robert Spire 3

Cataclysm of the Ancients – Robert Spire 4

Red Mist: Espionage Thriller

Vaporized

Vaporized II

SALIENT was edited by David Arden of
www.onlinebookservices.com

For Rochelle, my beautiful star, turning 6 in January.

SALIENT

*"A tiny blue dot set in a sunbeam. Here it is. That's where we live. That's home. We humans are one species and this is our world. It is our responsibility to cherish it. Of all the worlds in our solar system, the only one so far as we know, graced by life." – **Carl Sagan**

SALIENT

PROLOGUE

Mount Shasta, Mountains, California
September 16

MOUNT SHASTA'S SNOWY 14,179 feet high peak loomed skyward from the horizon, some one hundred or so miles distant. A sign on the side of the interstate stated they'd just entered the Cascade Range, Siskiyou County, California. The information post also confirmed that Mount Shasta was still a potentially active volcano, the second highest peak in the Cascades and the fifth highest in California.

"Wow, cool, isn't that something eh?" the brunette in the passenger seat said, turning to her girlfriend, Jessica.

"Yeah looks great Madison, a cold, spooky-looking mountain," Jessica said, placing a length of strawberry blonde hair behind her ear. "The view sure beats sitting in that real estate office back in Fairbanks though; and I've only been there five minutes," she added.

"Well, you can see where all the stories come from!" Tom, her part-time, on-off British partner said, looking up from the rucksack he was checking in the back of the Chevrolet Suburban.

"Dude, don't tell me you believe all that crap?" Conner said, turning his head away from the road for a second in order to project his voice over the sound of Lana Del Ray's *National Anthem*, pumping from the Chevrolet's stereo.

"You're always so sceptical about everything," said Madison, Conner's current girlfriend, who was seated next to him.

Conner shrugged. "Whatever, guys, you can save your bullshit scary stories for later when we're around the campfire!"

"Don't worry, I intend to," Tom said, his English accent dampened after three years at MIT, where he'd been studying physics and astronomy.

The four of them had been travelling along Interstate 5 after stopping in the town of Redding, about an hour earlier, for a coffee and burger break. Outside the window, on their left, the pine-covered mountains of the Shasta Trinity National Forest – California's largest national forest – rose up from the valley floor.

"How much longer is it, Conner?" Tom asked, as he finished checking through the contents of his backpack.

"The campsite's off the A10, about half an hour past the town of Shasta. It's probably going to be closed, but that's what makes this trip more fun, we'll be pretty much alone," Conner shouted back.

"What do you mean closed?" Jessica asked, from the rear.

Tom laughed. "Well, not really closed, just not fully open. It's only a campsite, it's just that legit visiting times usually finish September fifteenth I think."

Jessica rolled her eyes. "Well it's the sixteenth today, idiots!"

"Exactly, we'll be fine, just means fewer people, far more romantic," Tom replied.

"Well I hope we can get in," Jessica said.

Conner continued along the interstate which, despite the many hours of driving, didn't seem to be taking them any closer to Mount Shasta. Beautiful vistas of the park's pine forests stretched out on either side of the highway, which compensated any traveller's journey through the mountain range. After a short while, an interstate sign confirmed they were now on the Cascade Wonderland Highway, which twisted and turned northwards as it tracked the Sacramento River that meandered along below on their right side.

The time was approaching five p.m. and after another forty-five minutes of driving they reached the town of Mt. Shasta, just as the mid-September sun started to dip low on the horizon, its last rays illuminating the snow flanked sides of the mountain in a golden hue.

"It does look stunning," Jessica said, before sipping her bottled water.

"And a little eerie," Madison replied, surveying the high peak through a small set of high-powered binoculars.

"Shouldn't be long now, we'll be through town in no time and turning off onto the A10. Then it's only about a forty minute drive to the camp site. Hopefully, we can get the tents up before dark," Conner said, as he negotiated a sharp right-hand bend.

"Cool, we'd better, I don't want to be putting up tents in the pitch dark," Madison said.

"No way, screw that!" Jessica added.

"We'll get them up, stop worrying," Tom said, as he checked out the half-empty streets of the town. "Did you guys know that the total population of this place is only about three thousand?"

"Well I'm not surprised. The volcano looks beautiful, but what would you do here? Be as boring as hell after a while," Madison said, pushing her shoulder-length, dark hair behind her ear.

Conner turned off the main street, following a signpost to the A10 mountain road. As he slowed down to take the bend, they passed a gun store. Displayed outside were various stuffed animals; bear, elk, deer and one odd-looking creature that was standing bipedal, around eight feet tall. "Lol, what the hell is that," Jessica asked, pointing at the menagerie of animals outside the store.

Tom craned his neck to look out towards where Jessica was pointing, and then laughed. "That's supposed to be a yeti, you know Bigfoot. They've been spotted around here apparently."

"You're kidding right!" Jessica said.

"Oh jeez, of course he is. That's not a real Bigfoot. There's no such thing, just made up stories by assholes trying to make some bucks with nothing better do to!" Conner said.

Tom shrugged. "Who knows? People swear they have seen the creatures, but Conner's right. No real evidence has ever been presented to confirm their existence, and most of the stories are hoaxes, no doubt."

"Okay guys, can you shut up, you're beginning to freak me out," Madison said, turning around.

Conner manoeuvred the Chevrolet around a deep pothole that had formed in the road, continued to the junction, and turned right onto the A10 mountain road. Either side of the narrow road, the pine forest grew denser and stretched out like a carpet of green surrounding the steep snow-white sides of Mount Shasta, just a few miles distant.

Madison slid the window down, letting the cool September air rush into the truck. "Wow, can you smell that?" she said, referring to the refreshing fragrance of pine.

"Yeah, smells like my mum's bathroom freshener back home in the U.K.," Tom said, smirking.

After thirty minutes of driving along the mountain road, a yellow, and barely visible sign-post, confirmed that it was only 2.5 miles to the *Pine Crags Wilderness Campsite.*

"We're almost there, guys," Conner shouted.

They continued on for another fifteen minutes until finally, on the left, the road branched off. Another sign, pushed over to an angle of forty-five degrees, as if hit by something, announced that they'd reached the camp site.

Conner pulled into the large, empty parking area and killed the engine.

"Look at that, guys, this is what we came for," Conner said, looking out at their surroundings. Just beyond the hard natural earth parking lot was small lake, and beyond, pine-covered mountain peaks as far as the eye could see, all set against the backdrop of the vast volcano, which rose skyward half a mile or so away from their position.

"Wow, amazing! Well let's go find a suitable spot and get our tents up before darkness falls," Madison said, opening the truck door.

"Good idea," Tom said, "You ready, babe, let's go," he said to Jessica.

The four of them grabbed their backpacks from the back of the truck and headed off in the direction of a small hut, near the edge of the lake. The hut was empty and locked with a *Season Closed* sign across the Perspex screen where the campsite warden would usually sit.

"Ah well, at least the stay won't cost us anything," Tom said, peering into the hut.

"If the showers don't work, we can always bath 'au natural' in the lake," Conner added.

"You got to be kidding! It'll be bloody freezing in there," Jessica replied, rolling her eyes.

"Come on, looks like a good spot over there," Tom said, pointing past the hut towards a clearing in the forest, fifty feet away, just shy of the lake.

The four of them headed towards the spot and as they got closer, a rancid smell became noticeable, overpowering the fragrant scent of pine.

"Jeez, it stinks," Jessica said, screwing up her nose.

"It sure isn't very pleasant," Tom said, trekking behind Conner to the clearing.

"Eew, we can't sleep here, it bloody stinks like something just died," Madison said.

They headed over to a large tree bordering the clearing. As they rounded it, a buzzing sound, increasing in volume, became evident.

"Ah shit! What the hell is that?" Jessica said, stopping in her tracks, snapping a hard twig underfoot as she did, the loud *crack* startling everyone.

On the ground, obviously dead by the way its neck was twisted at an unnatural angle, and partially covered in dry leaves, was a large, bloodied stag, the source of the stench.

"Stay there, guys," Tom said to Jessica and Madison as he and Conner walked over to the dead animal.

The buzzing was emanating from the hundreds of flies swarming over the exposed flesh of the stag, where its hind legs and abdomen had been ripped open by a wild animal, exposing what was left of its torn and shredded innards.

"Christ, a black bear you think?" Tom suggested, glancing up at Conner.

"Got to be, or a coyote maybe?"

Tom shrugged. "I've never seen a coyote taking down something this big before."

"Come on, let's get back to the girls, best not scare them," Conner added, as they turned and walked back to where the girls were waiting.

"We'll find another place to set up camp. It's just a stag, been dead for twelve hours or so. Some coyotes must have brought it down. Don't worry, once we have the camp fire going, they won't come anywhere near us," Tom said, trying to reassure the girls.

"We can go over there," Conner said, pointing to another clearing, about seventy feet farther along the lake edge.

As they walked alongside the lake, a distant cry from an animal or bird made its presence known from deep within the forest.

CHAPTER 2

TOM HAMMERED THE final tent peg into the ground, securing the second of the two *Ozark Trail* two-man tents that he and Conner had just finished erecting in the pine forest clearing. "Nice one mate, just in time. Sun is just about to disappear," Conner said.

"Well done, guys. At least that icky smell has gone," Madison said.

"Come on; let's get the fire going quick. I'll go search for some tinder," Jessica said, rubbing her hands together as she headed towards the trees that bordered the clearing, Madison following her.

"Help me get some stones for the fire," Conner said to Tom.

Tom was looking up towards the volcano and its snow covered sides, which were reflecting enough of the light that was left to illuminate the surrounding forest in an ethereal glow.

"Yep, sure," Tom said, peeling his eyes away from the surreal view.

The pair of them headed to the lake edge and found enough small boulders to arrange around a depression they'd found near the tents, to make a perfect fire.

Forty feet away, Jessica and Madison were in the forest gathering large twigs. They had a good armful each, but the fading light was making it difficult to see. "Come on, let's get back, I think we've enough here," Jessica said.

Madison nodded. As they turned to walk back, they heard a distant *crack* from deep in the forest, like a tree branch, or piece of wood snapping.

"What the hell was that?" Madison whispered.

"God knows. Probably just an animal," Jessica said. "Come on, let's get back and get the fire started," she added, as they both turned and headed back to the lake edge.

"Here you go, guys," the girls said, dumping the tinder they'd collected on the floor by the ring of boulders.

"Nice one," Tom said, grabbing the twigs and sticks and arranging them inside the stone ring. A few minutes later, he'd managed to set the smaller twigs alight and the tinder was now burning nicely, the flickering flames warming and bathing the four of them and the small clearing in an orange glow.

Tom opened two tins of baked beans and stirred them in a pan that was resting on a couple of flat stones and started to heat them up.

"So, come on, Mr. Englishman, tell us some stories about this place," Madison said, as she lit a Marlboro and took a long drag on it.

"Yeah, go for it," Jess said, as she shifted on the blanket that she and Madison were sitting on.

Conner rolled his eyes. "Hold on, I'm going to get us a couple of beers," he said, as he got up and headed over to the truck.

Tom finished stirring the beans and moved the pan out of the heat slightly. "Well, as you know, Mount Shasta is an active volcano, part of the so-called Pacific Rim of Fire. If that wasn't enough, there's plenty of weird stories connected with this place," he said, glancing up at the mountain.

"Well, go on, tell us some!" Madison said, leaning in towards the fire.

Tom gave the beans another stir. "Well, legends and mysteries abound in this place. There are records of hikers and campers feeling an ethereal aura when trekking near or around the mountain, and native people have always held the mountain as a sacred area.

"Well, all we've experienced so far is a nasty smell," Madison interrupted.

Jess giggled. "Tell me about it!"

Tom continued. "UFO proponents are said to believe a secret alien base is located deep within the mountain."

"That's just silly!" Madison said.

Conner returned with four cans of Budweiser. "Actually, there's some support for that theory," he said, sitting down next to Madison and handing them each a can. "A chap called Kenneth Arnold was flying his light aircraft near Mount Rainier, along the crest of the Cascade Range back in, I think 1947, when he spotted nine high-speed objects, which he described as, *flying like a saucer would*. His report made international headlines at the time."

Tom opened his beer and took a gulp, before turning to his friend. "That's correct; I didn't expect you to have known that. There are also some, admittedly strange sects who believe the mountain is even an entry point into a fifth dimension. Many strange, pulsating lights have been reported over the past five decades by some very credible witnesses."

Jessica suddenly shivered. "Now you're freaking me out," she said, opening her beer.

Tom shifted the pan over the flames to give the beans one last blast of heat, before serving them. "In 1931, a forest fire swept across Mount Shasta, but was apparently stopped from advancing by a mysterious fog that appeared from nowhere. Interestingly the weird fog created a fire-line demarcation of charred forest, which was curved in direct correlation with the Central Time Zone line."

"Hmm, that's a bit freaky," Madison said, looking at Jess.

"But, the most worrying fact for us, tonight, guys is that we might be sharing the forest with…Bigfoot. Many sightings have been reported on Mt. Shasta. It's believed by many to be the hiding place home of the mythical creatures."

"Now you're freaking me out, too Tom. Don't be an asshole!" Jessica said.

"Now that's BS," Conner said. "If that was the case they'd have a real stuffed Bigfoot, Sasquatch or whatever you want to call it back down at the gun store, not a silly fake one."

Tom shrugged. "I'm just reciting the stories," he said, grabbing the pan from the fire and serving up four plates of hot beans for everyone. "Tuck in, guys."

The four of them ate in silence, apart from the odd crack and pop springing from the fire in front of them as the tinder burned.

"What's the time now, guys?" Madison asked, finishing a last spoonful of beans.

Tom checked his watch. "Coming up to ten."

"Blimey, that late already? What time are we setting off hiking tomorrow?" Jess asked.

"Let's try to get going around seven. It's going to be a long day," Tom said, finishing his beer.

"Well, I'm not going to get much sleep after those spooky stories you told," Jess said, glaring at Tom.

"Well you asked to hear them! Besides, they're only stories," he said.

"Chill out, honey. When Tom pulls you in that tent and uses his British charm on you, you'll be asleep in no time!"

"Funny," Tom said, picking up a small twig and throwing it across the fire at Madison.

"Stop scratching my ankle with your toes, please," Jessica said, prodding Tom in the stomach.

"Hey, it was an accident, babe," Tom replied, shifting in the twin person sleeping bag.

"I can't sleep," Jess whispered.

Tom cuddled up, kissed Jessica on the lips, then pulled away. "Hmm, maybe you need a bit more action to help you sleep?" he said.

"Hmm, the only action I need is for my eyelids to close," she whispered. "What time is it anyway?"

Tom checked his watch. "One forty."

Suddenly, from somewhere outside the tent, a low-pitched growl was audible for a brief moment, followed by a couple of thuds, and the sound of a dry twig snapping.

"What the fuck was that?" Jessica whispered, her green eyes wide-open with fear.

There was another flurry of heavy footfall, followed by a loud, hollow, *thud...thud...thud*, as if someone, or something was whacking the trunk of a large tree with a baseball bat.

"Shhh," Tom whispered, raising his finger to his lips.

Jess stared at him, her eyes fearful.

Suddenly, there was a loud pounding on the ground right outside, followed by an eerie, low Neanderthal-sounding growl.

"Is it a bear?" Jess whispered, petrified.

Tom edged slowly to the end of the tent, and very quietly, started to unzip the entrance, bottom to top.

A three-quarter Moon bathed the clearing and pine forest beyond in light, giving quite good visibility. Everything appeared normal at first, until his eyes focused on a large, dark mass which he'd first thought was part of a huge tree at the edge of the clearing. *Were the shadows from the trees branches playing tricks?*

Then he saw something, a pair of eyes, white and green, eight feet or so off the ground. Tom felt his knees shake as he tried to fathom out what the object was that he was looking at. *What the hell?* He said to himself, as he traced the outline of a large, hairy animal, which was standing upright on two legs in the shadows of the tree. Could a bear do that?

He quickly zipped the tent flap back up and quietly moved back over to Jessica. "I think it's a bear, we...we need to stay calm, don't move," he whispered nervously, while reaching into the side pocket of his backpack for his hunting knife.

Suddenly, there was another growl, this time much louder, and coming from just outside the tent. The growl was followed by the sound of material ripping...tent material. And then a blood curdling scream pierced the night air.

"Fuck, that's Madison!" Jessica screamed.

"Jesus," Tom replied, gripping the knife tighter in his right hand. "We need to leave the tent. When we do, I want you to run. Run for the car and don't look back! Here's the keys, get in, lock the doors, and wait for me," he whispered.

Madison screamed again, but this time the scream was different, more muffled, and weaker.

Tom unzipped the tent flap and he and Jessica crawled out, a stench of rotting flesh greeted them as they inhaled the cool night air.

The scene in front of them defied all rationality. A huge, muscular creature, covered in matted, brown hair and a large ovoid head, was standing upright, its arm held out, and its hand gripping Madison around her neck. Madison's legs were dangling beneath her, frantically kicking the air.

"Run for the car," Tom shouted to Jess, as he crouched, frozen to the ground at the sight in front of him. His brain was telling him it had to be a bear, but his eyes were looking at something different.

Jessica scrambled off in the direction of the car, her hands across her mouth, as she tried to stifle her cries.

The creature cocked its head over to one side, and stared directly at Tom, its green eyes appearing luminous under the bright Moon. A sickening crack followed, as it snapped Madison's neck with one quick jerk of its huge, hairy hand.

Then, from the side of the tent, Conner appeared, holding a thick piece of tree branch, which he used to whack the creature across its neck.

No way, Tom thought, as he instinctively ran over to help his friend. He plunged the hunting knife he was holding into the creatures flank, but its hair was so thick he had no idea if the blade had gone in.

The creature twisted its upper body towards Tom and let out an ear-piercing, guttural scream that made Tom's neck hair prick up in sheer terror.

The creature then yanked the knife out, grabbed Conner, and proceeded to batter his head hard against the ground. Conner didn't stand a chance. The creature was mercilessly smashing his head and torso against the ground as if he were a rag doll.

"Run...fucking run, mate," gurgled Conner, from his bloodied mouth.

The creature then twisted its upper body towards Tom and let out another ear-piercing scream that sent an icy shiver racing up Tom's spine.

Tom glanced towards the truck, which was in darkness. There was no sign of Jessica. He hoped she'd managed to get inside. He was about to run in the direction of the parked vehicle, but feared he wouldn't make it, so he turned and sprinted as fast as he could towards the river bank, leaping into the fast flowing river as he reached the edge, without looking back.

He winced in pain as the freezing water enveloped him, the fast-moving river carrying him downstream.

CHAPTER 3

SEARCH FOR EXTRA TERESTRIAL
INTELLIGENCE (S.E.T.I)
Mountain View, California

September 17, 3 A.M.

PROFESSOR FREDERICK BECK was seated in front of a large array of computer monitors, drinking a mug of coffee that had gone cold about an hour earlier, when the screen to his left, monitoring close-Earth radio signals started going crazy.

Beck, who'd been volunteering his time at the SETI institute for the last thirty-six months, spun his leather chair towards the screen to take a better look, spilling half the tepid contents of his cup in the process.

The screen confirmed a high-frequency burst signal, which wasn't in the usual frequency range. A signal that hadn't been detected before, and importantly, one that had been filtered out against the randomised, natural signals that occur in nature. He pulled his chair closer and stared at the monitor in disbelief. Not since the *Wow* signal had he seen anything that looked like this before. The signal was repeating and artificial in nature.

Beck was still a young physics undergrad when the *Wow* signal, a strong, narrowband radio signal, was received on August 15, 1977, by Ohio State University's Big Ear radio telescope in the United States, which was at the time used to support the search for extra-terrestrial intelligence. The signal appeared to come from the constellation Sagittarius and bore the expected hallmarks of extra-terrestrial origin, but unfortunately it was never detected again.

A number of hypotheses were advanced as to the source and nature of the signal, but none of them achieved widespread acceptance.

Atmospheric twinkling, or a rotating lighthouse-like source, a signal sweeping in frequency, or a military source had all been possible candidates for the signal.

The theory Beck had preferred, if the signal wasn't genuine, was that it had been an Earth-sourced signal that simply got reflected off a piece of space debris. Could the signal they were now looking at be the same?

"Lucy, you might want to get over here, now!" Beck said, calling his colleague Dr Lucy Davies.

Lucy who was studying some gamma ray burst data at the opposite end of the room, looked up and removed her reading glasses. "Say again?"

"We've picked something up. You need to see this," Beck shouted from the bank of screens.

Lucy dropped the paperwork she was holding, rushed over and sat on the chair next to Professor Beck.

She stared at the screen for a short while before whispering, "Double *wow!*"

Professor Beck started frantically hitting the keyboard in front of him. "I'm filtering out all the usual Earth-based signals and natural suspects now," he said, hitting the Return key.

The monitor turned black briefly, equations and text streaming down the screen, before it returned to the pulse graph showing the signal, its strength, and frequency, the data displayed at the bottom of the screen.

"Filter it further to locate the source," Lucy said, pushing her long dark hair behind her ear, her brown eyes darting between the screen and Professor Beck.

"I'm on it," Beck said, tapping away at the keyboard.

The SETI software started tracking the signal, analysing Earth's closest stars first, starting with Proxima Centauri, Rigil Centaurus and Barnard's Star, before moving onto the more distant stars. The screen suddenly went blank and an error message flashed up, before quickly vanishing again.

Dr Lucy Davies glanced at the professor, who was looking at the screen, mildly confused.

Another message popped up –

RECALCULATING SIGNAL SOURCE.

The screen flickered, before the message – *Signal source located*, scrolled across the screen.

"And," Lucy said, as if the computer were teasing her.

Source - Mount Shasta, Cascade Mountains, Northern California, U.S.A.

"What the hell?" Professor Beck whispered, staring at the screen, his jaw dropping open in disbelief.

"We need to get ATA on to it, and call NASA to get the signal verified," Lucy said, shaking her head, referring to ATA, or the *Allen Telescope Array*, a radio telescope array situated at the Hat Creek Radio Observatory, some 290 miles northeast of San Francisco, dedicated to astronomical observations and a simultaneous search for extra-terrestrial intelligence.

"Right away," the professor said, picking up the phone on the desk in front of him, and hitting the direct dial button.

CHAPTER 4

TOM SWAM TOWARDS the river bank and clawed at the muddy grass as he dragged himself out of the icy water. He had no idea how far the river had taken him, but he guessed it must have been half a mile at least. Clear of the water, he rolled onto his back to catch his breath, panting with exertion. He had to find Jessica, and wondered how far from the road he was. His head spun with questions, questions he didn't have answers to.

The billions of visible stars twinkled in the crystal clear night sky above. Alnitak, Alnilam and Mintaka, the three bright stars that made up Orion's Belt were particularly noticeable. Tom had studied the triple star system for one of his projects. Although the stars were some 700 light years from Earth, they were a hundred-thousand times the luminosity of the Sun, hence their brightness.

The fear from what he'd just witnessed flooded back into his head like a tidal-wave. Could he really have just seen a Bigfoot? Or had it been a large, crazed bear? He felt confused, unsure of what he'd really witnessed. Tom tore his watery eyes away from the shimmering stars and looked around the river bank and dark woods beyond. Had the creature stalked him? Was Jess still alive? "Fuck!" he whispered under his breath, as he got to his feet, rubbing his arms and hands together in a vain attempt to warm up.

All his learning and research at the Massachusetts Institute of Technology, where he'd studied physics after deciding to head to the U.S.A. once he'd completed a law degree in the U.K. hadn't prepared him for this. He was planning for a future career in planetary science and his main interest, the search for exo-planets, particularly planets capable of harbouring life outside our own solar system. He had an open and inquisitive mind, but his studies and research had never prepared him for an encounter such as this. *It was extraordinary*, he thought, as he shivered and ran towards the tree line in search of the road.

Jessica was shaking uncontrollably and huddled down in the foot-well of the passenger seat inside the SUV, too scared to look out the window. Not that she could see much through the dark, tinted glass anyway. What the hell had just happened? She couldn't fathom what she'd just witnessed. The last image she had was of Madison, being held by the neck by what? Had it been a bear or something that shouldn't exist?

She felt herself hyperventilating and covered her mouth with her hands. *Concentrate on breathing*, she told herself as she felt another wave of panic wash over her. The creature was still out there. What if it could smell her? She didn't want to die. Not now, not like this, surely to God.

Jessica felt her heart rate quicken, and then she blacked out.

Tom reached the tree line, stopped, peered into the darkness beyond the trees, and listened. Apart from the distant hoot of an owl, the forest was quiet. He thought back to the journey up, and tried to form a picture in his mind of the Sacramento River, and the road up to the campsite. The river had been on their right side on the route up. Thankfully, he'd exited the river on the correct side. He headed into the woods, moving slowly in a direction that should take him towards the road.

Tom had been walking for around twenty minutes when he heard something; a rustling, and a twig snapping somewhere in the forest. He froze, his heart pumping in his chest like a bass drum. He listened, trying to determine if it was just an ordinary forest animal or a larger creature. The forest fell silent again, unusually silent. He waited for five minutes or so, remaining motionless, but the sound didn't return. Petrified and cold, he moved forward as stealthily as he could, over the dry forest ground.

Another twenty minutes walking and he saw a strip of light through the trees. He squinted and focused on the strip, before realising it was the moonlight reflecting off the surface of the road. *Thank God*, he thought, as he moved as quickly as he dared through the trees, crossing the one-hundred feet or so distance to the road. He made it, scrambled down a small bank, and stepped onto the asphalt. As expected, the road was deserted, and the dark forest either side freaked him out. But at least he felt a little safer all of a sudden, and thankfully the road was lighter, the surface lit by the moonlight from the full Moon above. He checked the time; it was 03.40. It was easy to work out which way to go. The road was on a slight incline, and he knew it led down towards the town of Shasta and up towards the campsite. He couldn't leave Jessica alone, so headed up, hoping she was still safe, and waiting for him in the SUV, somewhere near the campsite entrance.

CHAPTER 5

NASA AMES RESEARCH CENTER
Moffett Field, California
September 17, 6 A.M.

NASA EXOPLANET SCIENTIST, Professor Hans Willems, picked up the phone. He was seated at his desk, just finishing a report on the latest Earth-like planet that NASA's Kepler spacecraft had discovered orbiting Proxima Centauri, a star just 4.25 light-years away. The newly-discovered exoplanet was Earth-like, and orbited within its sun's habitable, or goldilocks zone, the distance from its star where life can comfortably exist. He was about to go home for the evening, but his curiosity got the better of him. "This better be good," he said, upon answering the phone.

"Evening Hans, its Fred over at SETI," Professor Beck said, clearly excited about something.

Professor Willems listened to his colleague as he explained what the SETI systems appeared to have picked up, the frequency and apparent source of the signal.

"Are you sure about this?" Willems asked, suddenly forgetting about the 'date night' he'd arranged with his wife of eighteen years.

He swivelled his chair forty-five degrees and rolled it over to the desk situated below the bank of computer monitors fixed to the wall opposite and pulled the wireless keypad towards him. He keyed in a code that allowed him to use NASA's computer systems to analyse the signal, its source, and any other interesting data.

As NASA's *Titan* supercomputer crunched the data, Willems considered the ramifications if the signal was genuine. Before he had time to think about the protocol following the detection of a signal from outer space, the screen in front of him started streaming data, confirming signal source, strength, and frequency. It's chances of being a naturally occurring signal, placed at 0.012%.

Willems stared at the screen, his eyebrows raised, his jaw slowly dropping open.

Tom rounded a bend in the road and caught glimpse of the wooden totem poles that marked the gated entrance to the campsite. Pine trees stretched out either side like a solid wall in the darkness. When he finally reached the entrance to the campsite, his nerves were frayed, and every sound that emanated from the forest sent a shiver down his spine. He hadn't seen any vehicle lights on the road during his trek up through the forest and figured that Jessica must still be here unless she'd driven off whilst he'd been in the river, which was possible.

Tom crouched down by one of the large totem poles and peered into the camp site area, hearing the river flowing by in the distance. Apart from an early morning breeze rustling through the pine trees, all was still. He needed to move farther into the site to get a proper view of the car park area off to his left. He crept in, glancing every few seconds to his right, where the attack had taken place an hour or so earlier.

A silhouette of Conner's stationary SUV came into view, parked up in the spot where they'd left it. Had Jess even made it to the vehicle? A wave of nausea washed over him as he feared the worst. He pulled out his smartphone and found it wasn't functioning, water damaged from his earlier spell in the river.

He crept towards the vehicle, using the mature trees as cover to keep himself as hidden as possible, hoping the creature had gone. He made it to the thick trunk of a spruce tree and looked around. The SUV was twenty feet away, parked in a clearing, at the far edge of the camp site's parking area.

He took a deep breath and darted across the open space to the truck, crouching down by the passenger side wheel for cover. He reached up to the door to try it, but it was locked.

Tom cursed under his breath. Jessica had the keys, and he didn't have a spare. He scuttled around the front of the vehicle and tried the driver's door, also locked.

He looked to his left, towards the small hut they'd passed on the way to the clearing where they'd set up the tents. The area was well lit by the Moon, but he saw nothing, apart from trees and shadows, the only sound came from the river gushing by a short distance away.

Tom rose to peer in through the SUV's tinted, glass driver's window to look for Jessica, cupped his hands and stared into the vehicle. As his eyes adjusted, he made out the balled up figure of Jess in the foot-well of the passenger side.

A wave of relief rose inside him and he went to walk back around the front of the car to the passenger side, but froze in his tracks as he saw the silhouette of something large, standing on the tree line, looking directly at him.

CHAPTER 6

Pine Crags Wilderness Campsite, 6.40 A.M.

TOM FELT HIS legs turn to jelly. A second later, he heard a loud *click*, like the sound of a branch snapping, and the dark shape moved towards him. Something sounded familiar about the sound however. It wasn't the sound of a branch snapping, but of a gun being loaded.

"What the hell is going on here boy?" A man's voice boomed from the tree line.

Tom strained his eyes as he felt a palpable wave of relief wash over him. "Don...don't shoot," he said, as he moved back round the front of the vehicle.

A man dressed in dark clothing, holding a sawn-off shotgun, stepped out from beside a large tree. Tom immediately noticed a five-pointed star fixed to his jacket, glinting in the moonlight.

"I'm Sheriff Rob Garland, Mount Shasta Police Department. Keep your hands up, boy. What the hell are you kids doing out here? Damn camp site has been closed for a week."

"Yep, we know it's a bit late in the season, but there's no need for the gun. I need help. My girlfriend's in the vehicle. We were attacked…"

"Attacked?" The sheriff said, moving closer to Tom, shotgun still aimed at him.

Tom took a deep breath, and trying to compose himself said, "I think it was a bear, something larger, I'm not sure!"

"Are you taking the piss, boy? If you college kids are playing pranks on each other do it in your own backyards not out here."

Tom rubbed his arms, he was freezing. "It sounds crazy I know. We set up camp over there," he said pointing. "My two friends were attacked. Their bodies are over there. There's also a large stag carcass, looks as if it's been freshly killed by something large."

The sheriff looked towards the woods and a small clearing not far from the lake. "Are you being serious?" The sheriff said, noticing the look of anxiety on Tom's face.

"Yep, I swear...."

"Well you better not be fooling around kid," The sheriff said, cutting him off.

"At least let me check on my girlfriend," Tom said, gesturing toward the car door. "It's locked and I don't have the keys. Jess isn't responding."

The sheriff pressed his face up against the passenger window for a second, then stepped back, walked briskly around the car, and over to the driver's window. He then held his shotgun with both hands, as if he were gripping a pole, and slammed the end of the barrel into the driver's window, shattering it with one blow. "Go get her," he grunted.

Tom leant across to the foot-well where Jess was still huddled into a ball. The noise from the shattered window must have woken her. She looked up at him, trembling, mascara smudged on her cheeks, and her eyes open wide in fear. "To...Tom?" she whimpered.

"It's okay honey. I came back, the sheriff is here too. We're safe," he said, hugging her as best he could from his horizontal position.

With Jessica out of the vehicle and slightly calmer, they followed the sheriff over to where the attack had taken place.

"Are you sure you're okay?" Tom whispered to Jess, as they passed the small, wooden ticket hut.

Jess nodded. "I need to know what happened to them."

They approached the area where they had erected the tents, allowing them to clearly see the second tent, which had been ripped to shreds. The sleeping bags and remains of Madison's and Conner's backpacks lay strewn over the ground.

"Is this your friend's tent?" the sheriff asked, upon reaching the spot, realising that something odd had clearly taken place.

Tom nodded, seeing no evidence of Madison's and Conner's bodies.

The sheriff looked at them. "You expect me to believe that your friends have been taken by a bear, or something larger?" he said, grinning slightly, his tone harsh once again.

Tom scrutinised the ground around the tent as he replayed the attack in his mind, recalling the thing smashing Conner's head against a rock. He found the rock, partially hidden by some torn canvas from the tent, Conner's blood still clearly visible splattered over it.

"Over here," Tom said, showing the sheriff the blood stained rock. "And here," he added, spotting a set of two-foot wide drag marks, barely visible on the hard ground, disappearing into the woods.

The sheriff knelt down to inspect the tracks. "Okay, I accept that something odd has occurred here, but I can't guess at what," he said, looking into the trees. "Come on; let's get back to my vehicle. I'll radio for assistance and get you two back to town for some medical help and food."

CHAPTER 7

THE SHERIFF DROVE Tom and Jessica back down the mountain to the town of Shasta. They were both now seated in a small, but functional and warm interrogation room in the Mount Shasta Police Department in the centre of town. The clock on the wall had just ticked to 07.50.

"You kids must be wrecked. Here's some coffee. Breakfast is on its way," a female officer said to them, as she handed them both a mug of hot coffee. "I'm Lieutenant Jo Rogers," she said, smiling.

"Thank you," Tom said, warming his cold hands around the hot mug.

"We'll need to take statements from you once you've had breakfast, while events are still fresh in your minds. Then you'll be free to get some rest. Is that okay?" she said, glancing at them both in turn.

"Sure," Tom replied, wearily.

Lieutenant Rogers nodded and left the room.

"I still can't believe what happened to us," Jessica said, her eyes glazed. "Why didn't we just stay at home and have that dinner party we originally planned?"

Tom shook his head. "I agree, it's difficult to accept what we saw. I mean, I don't even know what we saw. If they never find the bodies or any evidence of that thing, who is going to believe us?" he said, taking a gulp of coffee.

The female officer returned with a cooked breakfast of eggs over easy, hash browns, beans, and streaky bacon.

"Oh, you don't happen to have any rice do you?" Tom asked.

"Rice?" the officer asked.

"To put this in," Tom said, holding up his waterlogged smartphone. "It might help!"

The officer smiled. "Sure, I'll go get some," she said.

"Well, it worked for me once when I dropped my phone down the toilet."

The officer raised her eyebrows and left the room.

Tom and Jessica ate in silence; their plates empty in no time.

Not long after they finished eating, the female officer returned with the sheriff, a small Dictaphone and a couple pads of notepaper in her hand.

"Okay, we need to take some details of what happened last night. We're treating this as a missing person's case at the moment but the things might change as the investigation progresses. There's no need to involve attorneys at the moment, but of course, you have the right to an attorney should you both wish. Do you understand?"

Tom looked at Jess and nodded. "We both understand. We'll just tell it as it happened. We don't need lawyers…yet," he said.

Jess nodded in agreement.

It took an hour for them to both tell the officers what they knew, from the moment they'd left their homes early yesterday morning, to the moment the attack had happened.

The female officer looked at the sheriff and back at the two of them. "Are you sure you don't want to....to change your statements in any way?" she asked.

Tom shrugged. "Nope, that's exactly what happened."

Jess nodded.

"Well, it's a little hard to believe, but if you say that's what happened, that's what happened, I guess," the female officer said, clearly sceptical.

"So, are we free to go? We really need to get some sleep," Tom asked.

"I guess so. I'd advise you to get a room here if you can. Save you driving all the way home. We'll send someone back to pick your vehicle up. All we ask is that you don't leave the State. We'll need to speak to you further once the investigation is underway. We will be sending out a search team shortly to look for your friends," she said. She reached into the pocket of her blue shirt and pulled out a card. "Here, call me if you think of anything else; any other detail," she said, slipping the card across the table towards Tom.

"Thanks," Tom said, as he and Jessica stood up to leave.

"Hold on a minute, Mr. Bishop," the female officer said, as she stood and left the room.

Tom felt his heart sink.

Lieutenant Rogers returned. "You forgot this. Nice idea with the rice, but it doesn't seem to have worked," she said, handing Tom his phone back.

"Oh! Well, thanks for trying anyway," Tom said, as he and Jess headed for the corridor and the way out.

Lieutenant Rogers looked at Sherriff Garland. "Do you believe them?"

Garland scratched his stubbly jaw. "Do I hell," he replied. "Come on; let's get the search party underway. Something happened up there for sure, but attacked by something that looked like a bear, but was bigger; really?"

"Well, there have been stories, of Bigfoot being spotted around here."

Garland shook his head. "Don't you start! Let's get back up there. We'll probably find out they were all smoking some strong grass, after which their friends wandered off to shag in the woods and became lost."

CHAPTER 8

"WHERE ARE WE going?" Jess asked, as she followed Tom out of the police station. He turned right, and was heading out of town, towards the mountain road.

"I want to speak to the owner of that hunting shop we passed on the way up."

"What, the owner of the creepy store with all the stuffed animals outside?" Jess asked, trying to catch him up.

"Yep,"

"Oh, bloody hell, can't we just go home?"

"Home?! Jess, our friends were just slain in front of us by a freaking creature that shouldn't exist, and you want to go home? I need to go to that store, ask the owner some questions."

"Okay, okay," Jessica replied, as they both walked along the street to where the shop was located, just before the bend where the road snaked up the mountain.

Ten minutes later they reached *Casey's Hunting Lodge*. And Tom looked up at the large, and clearly fake, stuffed Bigfoot. It looked nothing like the thing they'd seen last night. This looked more like an ape, whereas the thing they'd seen last night was more a cross between a bear and a human.

"I can't look at it. Let's go in," Jessica said.

They weaved their way through the large collection of stuffed animals, which were fixed to wheeled platforms for ease of movement, and entered the store.

A bell *dinged* above them as they opened the door, alerting the shop owner to their presence.

A man in his mid-thirties appeared from behind a long counter. "Howdy, folks," he said, eyeing them both with dark, beady eyes.

The shop was fairly dark inside, and the walls covered with moose, stag, and deer heads, their antlers protruding like old tree branches into the space, cobwebs coating most of them.

"What can I do you for?" the guy asked.

Below the mostly wooden counter, glass cabinets were filled with hunting guns and knives.

"Looking for a hunting weapon?" the guy asked, looking at them both in turn.

"Maybe," Tom said. "First, I just wanted to ask you about the stuffed Bigfoot you've got out there," he said.

"Old Sally? Ah, she's not for sale I'm afraid," the guy said, smiling.

"Sally?" Jess repeated.

"Sally Sasquatch. We've had her for thirty years, but she ain't for sale I'm afraid," he repeated.

"It's okay. We don't want to buy it," Tom said.

The guy shrugged. "What can I do for you then?"

"This is going to sound a bit odd, but we were camping last night up at Pine Crags Campsite and we got attacked…our friends were killed, we believe, by a bear-like creature, possibly a Bigfoot."

The guy stared at them in silence for a few seconds. "You're shitting me," he finally said.

"I know it's hard to believe, but we did," Jessica said, sounding emotional.

"Wait here," the guy said, as he turned and disappeared into another room through an arch behind the counter. "Pa," he shouted. "You're gonna want to come down here and see these folks."

The guy reappeared. "My Pa is going to want to speak to you guys. Take a seat, please," he said, pointing to an old, worn leather sofa tucked away next to a large, carved wooden bison, at the rear of the store.

Tom and Jess walked over and sat down. Two minutes later an older man, in his mid-sixties, appeared. He had a white, stained polo-neck jumper on, ripped, worn jeans, and a cap with the motif *Monster Hunter* written on it.

He strode over to them. "Howdy, I'm Casey. This is my store. My son, Arran, tells me you spotted a Sasquatch last night," he said, speaking excitedly in a gruff voice.

Tom cleared his throat, before telling the man briefly what had happened.

"I'll be damned," Casey finally said. "You positive it wasn't just a bear? I've been out trying to capture one of those things for two decades, and now you tell me this happened right up the road. Unbelievable," he said, taking his cap off and shaking his head.

"It didn't look like any bear I've ever seen. We just need your help. I mean, the police are involved so I guess we shouldn't even be talking to you about it, but…"

"Well I'm bloody grateful you did. The police won't do a damn thing. They'll go and have a look, find nothing, and treat the case as missing persons, like the rest. It's happened before, all covered up, believe me. No, the best way to deal with this is to get up there and hunt for the creature and what's left…I mean, your friends, ourselves. I know what to look for and I've been waiting for a moment like this all my life. I've also got a good buddy, in the film business. He's been waiting to produce a documentary about Mount Shasta for a long time. This is the perfect opportunity. I mean, sorry about your friends an' all," he said, stopping to catch his breath and glancing at them awkwardly. "This story is too big to be hushed up. I need to call Dickie now. Please, don't go away. I'll be right back," he said, before rushing over to the counter and disappearing through the arch.

"Oh God, what have we done?" Jessica said.

Tom shook his head. "I didn't expect this. I just wanted to ask the guy if he'd ever heard any rumours about what we'd seen. Crap," Tom whispered.

Casey returned after a few minutes, talking excitedly on a mobile phone he had gripped in his large, leathery hand.

"Yeah, yeah, that's right, they're here now. Happened last night, just five, six miles from the store, base of the mountain. Yeah…yeah," Tom heard Casey talking rapidly.

Casey nodded. "Great, we'll see you all tomorrow evening then. Yep, we can meet here. Cheers, Richard."

Casey ended the call and pulled a chair over to the sofa. "Well, that was my old pal, Richard Armstrong. He's a Brit, just like you. Has his own small film crew, works for Channel Five, I think it is? He's an independent documentary filmmaker, and been dying to do a story about this location for years. He's buzzing with excitement, thanks to you guys and is going to get on a flight first thing in the morning," Casey said, grinning.

"Jesus Christ," Jessica said, looking at Tom.

Tom shook his head. "Well, at least it'll be a British documentary," he said, not knowing what else to say.

"So what do you plan on doing exactly?" Tom asked, after a few moments silence.

"Well, Dickie already has funding in place for the documentary, which means we can spend a week up in the mountains to try hunt down whatever you saw. Plan will be to try and capture it alive, and make ourselves rich and famous in the process. We will have heat-seeking equipment, motion sensors, the lot. Dickie gets his documentary, while we try to hunt and catch a real live Sasquatch," Casey said, his eyes sparkling with excitement.

"This is all too much," Jessica said, as she started sobbing.

Tom put his arm around her. "Come on, honey. What do you want to do? Do you want me to drive us back home?" he said.

"I don't know. I do feel bad leaving here knowing that Maddie and Conner are still out there somewhere in the forest."

"Listen, guys. Can I make a suggestion?" Casey chimed in. "Why don't you stay here tonight. You'll be in the safest place in town; I've got a small armoury here and spare rooms upstairs. Stay the night, meet my mate, Dickie Armstrong tomorrow, and then decide what you want to do. You're both too tired to drive all the way back now anyway. What d'ya say?"

Jess looked at Tom and shrugged.

Tom nodded. "Okay, it's a done deal. We'll stay here and sleep on things."

"A very wise decision. You'll not regret it. I know it's terrible what happened out there, but the best remedy for your grief will be to try to find that thing and lay your friends to rest properly," Casey said.

"I hope we're doing the right thing," Jessica said.

Tom shrugged. "We'll find out soon enough."

Casey looked at them both. "Well, follow me, I'll show you to your room."

CHAPTER 9

SEARCH FOR EXTRA TERESTRIAL
INTELLIGENCE (SETI)
Mountain View, California.

"WHAT THE HELL do you mean the signal is being transmitted from Mount Shasta to the Moon?"

Professor Frederick Beck awkwardly scratched his beard. "That's what the Allen Telescope Array confirms. We ran a full system check. Even NASA's *Titan* supercomputer confirms what we're seeing. There's no doubt, a signal has been detected at the 2999 gigahertz frequency. It's emanating from a glacial region at the base of Mount Shasta, Cobalt Ridge to be precise, which terminates in or near the *Saha Impact Crater* on the Moon's far or dark side. Not only that, but a second signal has now been detected at the same location, at a frequency of 2990 gigahertz, which appears to be directed towards a region in the constellation of Cassiopeia, a main sequence star HR 8832, which is 21.25 light years from Earth," Beck said, looking drained and worried through lack of sleep.

"You're both kidding, right?" Frank Douglas, the tough-looking sixty-something, U.S. Military advisor said, placing his coffee cup down on the large oak table.

"I wish we were," Dr Lucy Davies said, sucking in a deep breath. NORAD, White Sands, and one of our AWACS have now all independently confirmed the signal. We seem to be dealing with the real deal here," she said, somewhat nervously.

"And the point source is local? You're absolutely certain about that, Dr Davies?"

Lucy slowly nodded her head at Douglas. "As certain as we can be."

"Jesus," Douglas replied, burying his head in his hands momentarily. "What do we know about that star system?"

"Dr Davies shuffled the papers she had on the table in front of her. "Well, we think the star is host to a rocky super-Earth, around one point six times the size of our planet, and there are a further three exoplanets, two of which are super-Earths, which orbit within the Goldilocks zone. There's one Jovian-type world too."

"And by Goldilocks I assume you mean a planet that orbits its sun within the habitable zone of space, like our own Earth?"

Dr Davies nodded slowly. "That's correct."

Douglas sighed again, heavily. "So I assume we need to invoke the post-detection protocols?"

Beck shifted on his chair. "You're referring to the protocols that were first drawn up in the 1980s, to help scientists in the United States and the Soviet Union share information about any potential SETI signals. The protocols were a bunch of guidelines drafted on the back of a cigarette packet over a couple of bottles of bourbon. Just guidelines for governments and scientists, rather than a global action plan for dealing with alien contact. All they basically say is, 'if you pick up a signal, check it out, tell everybody, and don't broadcast any replies without international consultation,' whatever that means," he said.

"That's all the protocols say, but they're better than nothing, and they have no force of law. The United Nations took a copy of the early protocols and filed them in a drawer somewhere, and that's as official as they ever got," Dr Davies added.

The four of them sat in silence for a few moments.

"So, can you tell us what happens from here?" Dr Davies asked.

"Well, the president's orders are to secure the site. Checkpoints are in the process of being set up for a one-hundred mile exclusion zone from the point source. The area needs to be off-limits to the public for now until we get an idea of what we're dealing with," Douglas said.

Dr Davies' smartphone suddenly vibrated on the table. It was her intern, Martha calling. She picked it up. "Sorry, Martha, I'm a little busy right now, can this wait?"

"Sorry, I appreciate that, but I think there's something you should know. The location we were discussing this morning. You'd better turn NCB News on right now," she said, before hanging up.

"Problem?" Beck asked.

"Can you turn that monitor onto NCB News station, quickly," Dr Davies said, nodding to Beck who was seated next to a large LED screen at the end of the table.

"Sure," he said, fiddling with the black control unit.

The monitor blinked on, and Beck found the correct channel. There was a reporter talking outside some kind of hunting shop, Mount Shasta clearly visible, its peak rising out of the pine forests in the backdrop, blue sky completing the scene.

"So what we know so far is that four campers intended spending the night up at the Pine Crags Wilderness Campsite, just ten miles or so from the town of Shasta here. Details are sketchy at the moment, but It appears that it will be a night they will never forget, as two of the campers were allegedly attacked by a bear-like creature that they say might have been the legendary Bigfoot, or Sasquatch, whatever you want to call it. Now, this place is known for its mysticism and travellers here have often reported feeling odd in this area and seeing strange lights in the sky, and there have been other sightings of the creature here, but this is the first report of an actual attack by a Bigfoot. If indeed that is what we are dealing with. We

don't know very much yet, but as you can imagine, Dean, speculation is rife, and this is a story that won't be going away anytime soon. Back to you in the studio."

"Wow! Well, thanks, Bernie, we sure will be keeping track as that story develops," Dean Duncan, the news anchor said, as the report ended.

The four scientists looked at the monitor, and then each other in stunned silence.

"This can't be happening, can it? I mean the signal and now this. A Bigfoot sighting – at the same location and time?" she said, in disbelief.

The military advisor shook his head. "Well, this really causes us problems. Any attempt to keep this entire thing low-key and people away from the area has been screwed up by this damn bullshit."

Lucy Davies shrugged and felt herself smirking. The entire thing was incredible. As if detecting a signal emanating from a glacial area of a mountain here on Earth, to the Moon and beyond to a star system twenty-one light years away wasn't enough. Now they had to deal with a Bigfoot sighting, an actual attack on some campers by such a creature, and all on the same day. Jeez, she loved her job, but her head was thumping.

"Okay, well we need to get back to Washington," the NASA scientist who'd been taking notes said, as he looked at his colleague, Frank Douglas.

Douglas grimaced. "We'll be in touch as soon as we know more, but from experience, this thing is going to get hot. Once the public are aware of what's going on, things could get quickly out of control. There'll be a lot of freaks out on the streets, doomsday placards, and all that stuff. We need to contain this story, try to avoid any panic and play this thing down until we know exactly what we're dealing with," Douglas said, as the pair of them grabbed their folders from the table and left the room.

Lucy looked at her colleague, Professor Beck. "Wow, come on, let's go to try and find out when the expedition to the glacier is going to take place. NASA and the government won't want to waste too much time getting this thing checked out," she said, her eyes twinkling with excitement.

CHAPTER 10

September 18

TOM SLIPPED OUT of bed and headed into the bathroom where he quickly shaved off four days-worth of stubble from his face, before jumping in the shower. He towelled himself dry, pulled on a pair of jeans and a clean, light blue cotton shirt, and crept out of the bedroom, leaving Jessica to sleep for a while longer.

Downstairs, Casey was already up, and in the process of sorting through items of equipment that he'd placed into small piles on the floor. Tom could see hunting knives, flares, camping equipment, and rifles with high-powered scopes. Casey sat down as Tom entered the room and started cleaning the reloading mechanism of one of the weapons, when he heard Tom and looked up. "Howdy! Did you sleep well, buddy?"

"Yeah thanks. I woke myself with a bad dream, but apart from that, I slept like a baby."

"Not surprised that you had nightmares after what you witnessed buddy. Anyway, I'm just getting some supplies ready. The Brits are paying for all this, so I sure as hell ain't going to hold back. Dicky and his team will be here in a few hours. We'll try to set off around lunchtime, so we can get up to the mountain before the government have time to set up proper security check points," he said, grinning.

"Morning," came Jessica's sleepy voice, from the archway just behind them, a moment later.

Tom turned to see her standing in her pyjamas, her blonde hair hanging messily, but sexily, across her forehead.

"Hey there, are you okay? I just came down. Didn't want to wake you," Tom said, walking over and kissing her on her lips.

"I'll get the wife to rustle you guys up some breakfast," Casey said, locking and unlocking the loading mechanism on the shotgun, with a satisfying *clunk*. "I was just telling Tom we aim to leave around noon, as I'm sure you guys could do with a big breakfast. It's probably going to be late afternoon before we get the chance to eat again," he said, placing the gun onto the counter.

"Sounds good," Tom said.

Jessica nodded. "I'll go take a shower then."

After breakfast, Tom asked Casey's wife if she could bury his smartphone in a pot of rice for a few hours. The brief spell at the police station hadn't been long enough to dry it out, or so he hoped. Casey's wife gave him a funny look, but carried out his request. He and Jessica then headed back to the room. It was still only 8.45 a.m.

Through the bedroom window, Tom could see the peak of Mount Shasta glistening in the early morning cloudless sky. However his gaze was suddenly distracted by a dark shape coming along the street below. He looked down and saw a dark green truck drive past, its noisy diesel engine spluttering black smoke as it headed up the road towards the camping area.

"Jeez, the military are here already," he muttered to Jess, as the truck rounded the bend and vanished up the mountain road.

Not long after the military vehicle had passed, Tom was outside studying the now very fake-looking Bigfoot model standing near the entrance to the store, when two brand-new looking Mercedes trucks pulled up onto the kerb and parked up. Large, bright yellow and blue lettering on the side confirmed the vehicles identity - Channel Five Productions, U.K.

A stocky chap in his mid-thirties, with short, blond hair and a friendly, trusting face jumped out, stretched his arms, and yawned; "Wakey, wakey," he said, either to himself, or another as yet unseen occupant inside the van.

He noticed Tom and walked over. "Hey, I'm Armstrong, Richard Armstrong. Say, you're not Tom Bishop, the guy involved in the grizzly bear-come-Bigfoot attack?" he asked, matter-of-factly.

"Um, yes, that's me. Well, it was my friends who were taken, I witnessed the attack," Tom said.

"Un-bloody-believable. Great to meet you Tom. I'm here courtesy of good old Channel Five. Where you from? I'm from Wales, lived in Penarth all my life," Armstrong said.

"Really? Well I was born in Cardiff, but lived in London for eight years, and have been over here the last four."

"Fantastic! I heard you studied physics at MIT? Perfect, lends an air of credibility to the documentary," Armstrong said, excitedly.

As he spoke, a tired looking brunette jumped out of the passenger side of the van.

"Meet Alicia, Alicia John, our make-up and lighting assistant," Armstrong said.

Tom smiled at Alicia, reached out and shook her hand.

"Hi Tom, it's nice to meet you," she said, yawning. "Excuse me, but I'm bloody knackered."

"Guys, I know you've come all the way out here to make a documentary on what happened, but this isn't a joke. I'm a pretty open minded guy, but I still can't get to grips with what happened last night, and you sure as hell won't need any makeup up there," Tom said.

Alicia pulled a face. "We always need make-up. Anyway, I'll leave you to it, boss," she said, looking at Armstrong, and jumping back into the truck.

"Don't worry, Tom; we're taking this stuff very seriously too. That's why I made sure I got over here as quickly as possible. We're here to make a documentary not a B-Movie."

At that moment a skinny, scruffy-looking kid with unkempt, ginger hair jumped out the back of the other truck, wearing torn jeans and a lumber-jack shirt. He looked excited and came running over to where the three of them were standing.

"Hey boss, boss, you're never going to guess what I just picked up. As you know, we've been eavesdropping on the U.S. Military radio channel to keep tabs on the security situation and..."

"Calm down, Bruce. This is Tom. Tom was involved in the attack last night. Tom, meet Bruce, my computer geek and general all-round tech wizard. Anything goes wrong, Bruce can fix it," Armstrong smirked.

Bruce reached for Tom's hand. "Ah, Tom, yes, very nice to meet you. I'm very sorry to hear about what happened to your friends up there. Unbelievable, but then there's lots of weird, unbelievable crap going on around here right now."

"So what did you find out, Bruce?" Armstrong asked, interrupting.

"Well, more weird shit really. Apparently, they've now detected some kind of signal that is being transmitted from the mountain to the Moon!" Bruce said, his eyes darting between Armstrong and Tom.

"Say that again, who's detected what?" Tom asked, his head starting to spin a little.

"Well, I just heard a conversation on the military channel I was tuned into. They were discussing a signal that SETI organisation, you know, the search for E.T., has detected, apparently originating from the mountain here and terminating on the Moon! I mean, how freaky is that with all this other crap that's going on?"

"Have you recorded the conversations?" Tom asked, intrigued.

"Damn right we have," Bruce said, looking at his boss.

"Well done, Bruce. Keep us informed, sounds interesting. We could include it in the story," Armstrong said.

"Okay, I'll get back to it, boss. Let me know when we're due to leave, as I'll want a wash and change of clothes before we head off," Bruce said, heading back over to the parked truck.

"Knowing a bit about your background, that must be of interest to you eh, Tom," Armstrong winked.

"The whole thing is crazy. Doesn't make sense, but if what I just heard is fact, then it's even more incredible than the events of the night on the mountain. I need to make some calls. See if any of my colleagues know anything about this," Tom said.

"Okay, where's my pal, Casey, is he up and about?" Armstrong asked.

"Yep, follow me. He's getting the supplies for the trip ready," Tom said, as they both walked into the store.

CHAPTER 11

THE TWO MERCEDES trucks pulled away from Casey's store forecourt, following two black Tacoma's, one being driven by Casey and the other by his son, Arran. Tom and Jessica were in the vehicle being driven by Arran. Tom glanced back at the store, now closed until they returned. The stuffed animals outside, including the fake 'Sally' Sasquatch, appeared to watch them leave, as if bidding them all good luck.

"I can't believe we're going back up there," Jessica said, expelling a little shiver as she snuggled up to Tom in the passenger seat.

"Yeah, I know what you mean. You know you didn't have to come with me, but I just can't let this go. What happened the other night was one thing, but now the detection of some kind of signal, if true, is something entirely different. There's no way I can't not investigate this further," Tom said.

"I know," Jessica whispered, accepting the situation.

Tom pulled out his smartphone, now working again after the rice trick, which must have absorbed whatever remained of the Sacramento River following his swim the night before, and checked the screen. There were no unread messages. He'd called his friend, Gerry, from MIT earlier, to ask him if he'd heard anything. Apart from the newsflash about the alleged Bigfoot attack, which was making the rounds, no mention had been made of any mystery signal mentioned by Bruce.

As expected, Gerry had been intrigued, and would try to find out what he could.

The Tacoma's accelerated up the mountain road towards the campsite, followed by Richard Armstrong and the Channel

Five film crew in the Mercedes trucks. The Sacramento River flowed lazily on their right, hiding the horror and mystery of the events from the night before. The pine forests of the National Park, home to more than just trees, deer, stags, and bear it seemed, stretched out either side of the road in a carpet of green.

A crackling voice erupted from the dashboard of the truck, and Arran yanked a radio that was attached to a bendy cable from the dashboard. "Good old-fashioned VHF CB," he said, answering the handset. "There's a military roadblock eleven miles ahead? Okay, Pa, so I'll follow you then," Arran said, replacing the CB.

"Is there a problem?" Tom asked.

"Not really Tom. As suspected, the military have set up a checkpoint on the main route up. Bruce, the Channel Five kid, has been listening in for us. My father knows an alternative route about five miles up from our current location, takes us through the forest and right up to the base of the mountain, bypassing the main road. Nobody will know we're there, unless they have radar or motion detectors."

"Sounds good," Tom replied.

They drove on for another ten minutes before Casey, in the lead Tacoma, braked and slowed. On the left side of the highway was a sloping grass bank, which appeared to lead nowhere. Casey drove his vehicle off the highway and down the bank, bringing it to a stop in an open area of grassland, some thirty feet away from the main road.

The radio sprang to life again, and Arran grabbed it from the dashboard. "Follow me down, but be careful, it looks steeper than it is," Casey's voice cracked from the device.

Arran manoeuvred the truck towards the bank and then drove, and half slid, down the bank and onto the flat grassy area, the two Mercedes trucks following slowly behind.

With all the vehicles parked up, Arran, Tom, and Jess got out. Casey was already standing alongside his vehicle, observing the forest through a pair of binoculars. Richard Armstrong, Bruce, and Alicia, the make-up artist, got out of the trucks and walked over to join them.

"Hey! Hello again, guys. It's a great day for an adventure eh?" Alicia said, smiling.

Armstrong strode over. "What's the plan then?"

Casey lowered the binoculars and handed them to Armstrong. "See that large fir tree directly ahead. Just to the left of it there's a small opening. It doesn't look large, but once we're through, it opens up to an old mining route that leads directly up to the side of the mountain. It's a bit bumpy, but we can avoid the military."

Armstrong looked through the binoculars, and after ten seconds or so nodded. "I see it. I like it," he said, handing the binoculars to Tom.

Tom looked through the binoculars in the direction of the large pine tree and noted a natural arch formed by the trees, which opened into a dark space beyond. The route was all but invisible to any vehicles that might pass along the highway.

"Where exactly are we heading?" Tom asked.

Casey stretched his arms. "Well, we'll be setting up base around mid-point between the camp site where you guys were attacked and the eastern flank of the mountain. It's a remote location, part of a hundred-year-old mining trail. The creature is unlikely to be anywhere near where we're going."

"Well I hope it's not anywhere near the mining trail either!" Jess said.

Tom felt his smartphone vibrate in his pocket and pulled it out. Gerry's name was displayed on the screen, and the start of a long text message appeared below it.

"Okay guys, let's get a move on," Armstrong said, heading back to the truck. "We'll follow you up."

Casey nodded and headed back over to his Tacoma.

"Don't worry Jess; these guys have enough firepower to stop a small army. Come on, I've just had a text through from Gerry," Tom said, as they followed Arran back to the vehicle.

Arran pulled off after his father, negotiating the vehicle around a fallen tree and proceeding under the low, pine tree canopy, and into the dark forest beyond. The film crew following slowly behind.

Tom pulled his phone out and opened the text message from Gerry.

JESUS, TOM, I CAN'T BELIEVE WHAT I'VE JUST BEEN TOLD. I CHECKED IN WITH MATT OVER AT SETI. HE CONFIRMED THAT A SIGNAL HAS INDEED BEEN DISCOVERED. THE SOURCE OF IT APPEARS TO BE A GLACIAL REGION ON THE EASTERN FLANK OF MOUNT SHASTKA, NEAR THE COBALT RIDGE GLACIER. THE SIGNAL APPEARS TO TERMINATE ON THE FAR SIDE OF THE MOON. BUT THERE'S MORE. A SECOND SIGNAL HAS JUST BEEN DETECTED CLOSE TO THE POINT AT WHICH THE FIRST SIGNAL TERMINATES, APPARENTLY DIRECTED AT THE CONSTELLATION OF CASSIOPEIA, 21 LIGHT YEARS FROM EARTH. TOM, THIS IS MASSIVE! THIS AND WHAT HAPPENED TO YOU GUYS LAST NIGHT, WHAT THE HELL IS GOING ON?!

Tom had to read Gerry's message twice to make sure he understood it properly. *This is crazy.* He showed the text to Jessica. "Unbelievable, eh? It confirms what Bruce overheard the military saying."

Suddenly, the truck hit something large, jostling them about in the seat. "Sorry, fallen tree; didn't see it," Arran apologised, slowing down a little.

They continued following Casey along the overgrown track, which was only just wide enough for the vehicles to travel along. Dense pine forest stretched out on either side of the hidden route, blocking out any view from main highway.

Arran's radio squawked to life and he pulled it from the dashboard. It was his father.

"Yep okay Pa, understood," he said, returning the handset.

"We're about two miles past *Pine Crags* now. There's an old mining hut and mineshaft coming up where an old wooden bridge crosses one of the tributaries of the Sacramento River. We need to stop and check the integrity of the bridge before proceeding over," he said.

Five minutes later, Arran pulled up behind his father's vehicle and cut the engine. They climbed out of the vehicle. A fragrant smell of fresh pine filling the air. The two Mercedes trucks stopped a short distance behind and their engines fell silent, allowing an eerie calm to descend. Just a faint gushing sound from the river a short distance away drifted across and permeated the surrounding forest.

Tom looked around. To their right was an old steel corrugated hut, overgrown with creepers that rose from the forest floor. Directly ahead he could make out the wooden bridge that traversed the small tributary of the Sacramento River, the reason they'd all stopped. Casey was already heading towards it.

"Come on, let's take a look," Tom said, taking Jessica's hand.

Arran grabbed his sawn-off shotgun from the front passenger seat and they followed him towards the bridge.

When they arrived at the old bridge, Tom could see the reason for Casey's concern. The old timber that formed the structure of the bridge had badly rotted and was covered in lichen for the most part. A sizeable hole where the timbers had completely perished had formed on the left side of the span, about quarter of the way across. There was no way the Mercedes trucks would get across.

"Any problem?" Richard Armstrong's deep Welsh voice made Tom and Jessica jump.

"Yeah, looks as if we might have to do a bit of repair work," Casey said, checking his watch.

"Well come on then, let's get it sorted," Armstrong replied, looking around them all, and the quiet, dense forest beyond.

CHAPTER 12

September 18, 3.45 P.M.

TWO AND A half miles southeast of their location, through the forest, a U.S. Army truck was parked on the side of the mountain highway; its eight occupants had been busy setting up a small temporary guard post together with a lever controlled barrier, which now blocked the route up. Four soldiers were offloading supplies from the rear of the truck; prefabricated sections that would form a small, but solid, and quickly erectable sleeping hut.

Two of the soldiers lit up cigarettes and started inspecting the side of the highway; the other two were still erecting what was about to become a guard post. One of the soldiers, with the name Ed Eastern sewn onto his green and brown forest-camouflaged jacket, pulled his standard issue Iridium Extreme PTT satellite phone from his belt, and tapped in a ten-digit number. The phone connected after five seconds. "Sir, its Sergeant Eastern. Check-point Alpha is secure and up and running. No problems as yet," he confirmed.

He nodded and ended the call. "They're setting up a check point close to the town, so we should be pretty quiet up here. Nobody gets through unless they have direct clearance from Major Grant himself," Eastern confirmed.

The other soldier nodded, adjusted his sunglasses and pulled his M14 from the gun rack. "No problem Sarge. Let's go and join the guys for a smoke," he said.

"That might do it," Casey puffed, as he tied the last piece of rope he had around the most appropriate diameter tree branches the five of them had helped gather from the surrounding area.

"Okay, I think we're just about done," he said, wiping mud from his hands on an old towel he'd taken from his truck.

Tom checked the time. It was approaching 2.30 p.m., the repair job having taken almost two hours to complete.

"Okay, let's get moving. Dickie, you take the trucks over first so we can keep an eye on the bridge," Casey shouted. "Once we're all over, we follow the winding route through the forest to our camp site. It's about four miles farther up."

"Okay," Armstrong said, heading back over to the truck. "You guys can cross by foot, keep the weight down."

Alicia and the two other members of the film crew; cameraman Doug Scott, and lighting technician John Adams headed back to the trucks. The two fresh-faced guys were in their mid-twenties, and virtually straight out of university. Getting to ride along on this trip was the experience of a lifetime for them.

"Bruce, you can follow me over," he added, as he jumped into the van.

Armstrong pulled the Mercedes up to the flimsy, wooden bridge, that must have been constructed using wood from the surrounding forest a hundred years ago, and very carefully edged onto it. Tom looked on. The drop to the river below was only ten feet or so, but if the thing collapsed, it would be the end of their trip, and the documentary, especially if all the filming and recording equipment ended up in the ravine.

The wooden bridge sections creaked as the heavy truck crept onto the structure. Casey and the others watching as the passenger side wheels rolled over the make-shift repair they'd carried out.

A loud and sudden, *crack,* emanated from one of the thinner branches as it snapped under the weight of the truck.

"Hold it!" Casey screamed, as he and the others checked to make sure the repair was going to hold. After inspecting the snapped section, Casey waved Armstrong safely over to the other side.

"Nice work, boys and girls," Casey said, a large grin returning to his face for the first time in two hours.

Bruce pulled up in the second truck and they waved him over. Casey and Arran then drove the Tacoma's over.

The journey thereafter was uneventful, apart from the vehicles having to swerve around the odd item of equipment left over from the route's one-hundred-year-old history as a copper mine. Old lanterns, steel buckets, and even an old, discarded ivy-covered mining cart littered the route. Tom assumed the tracks it had run on had long since been removed, the steel no doubt recycled into something else, or maybe stolen.

After another ninety minutes of driving up a fairly steep incline, they reached a small, level clearing in the forest. Mount Shasta rose up out of the pine trees almost directly ahead, its snow covered flanks in stark contrast to the surrounding forest, which stretched out like a verdant expanse to the small town and the valley below.

The three of them jumped out to stretch their legs. As Tom got out he noticed another old metal shack close to the edge of the forest, thinking it probably concealed the entranced to an old mineshaft. He made a mental note to go and take a closer look later on. The Mercedes trucks nosed up to each other and their engines fell silent a short distance away.

"Are you okay?" he asked Jessica, who'd been fairly quiet since they'd left the bridge.

"Yeah, I'm fine. No offence, but I'd just rather be home with my family right now to be honest," she said, forcing a smile.

"I know. I did give you the option to go home though," The excitement of Gerry's earlier text message was still fresh in his mind. Nothing else seemed important right now. He was hungry to find out what the hell was going on, and being close to the mysterious signal source overrode anything else.

"Let's just get this documentary done and have a bit of an adventure along the way. We'll be home in no time. The four of us came out here for adventure. We owe it to Conner and Madison to see this through don't we?" he said.

"I guess," Jessica said, rolling her eyes.

Armstrong and Bruce started unloading items of film equipment from the back of one of the Mercedes trucks. Tom watched them unload two movie cameras, complete with tripods, and some lighting equipment, which the brunette, Alicia, carefully lowered onto a flat area of grass. She then went back to the truck and fetched what looked like more film equipment and a couple of small trunks.

Casey removed a large hold-all from his truck and unzipped the top. Inside were a number of black radio-alarm clock sized devices. He tipped them out on the ground and arranged them in a row, twelve of them in all. "Guys, can you give me a hand with these," he asked.

"What are they?" Jessica enquired.

"Motion sensor detectors. We need to attach them to the trees, say four feet off the ground, at equal distances around the clearing. They will pick up anything of significant size that approaches the camp," he added.

Jess looked at Tom. "I hope he's not seriously expecting anything to turn up?" she said, anxiety returning to her voice.

"Don't worry; it will help alert us to any animal, especially bears, that might stray too close to the clearing. I seriously can't imagine that thing showing up again, but if it does we've got guns this time to deal with it if necessary," Tom replied, trying to allay Jess' fears.

He wasn't surprised she was frightened; he wasn't exactly feeling relaxed by any stretch of the imagination, but his scientific mind was ruling over his emotions and doing a good job of suppressing most of his fear.

An hour later and Casey and his son had set up all the motion detectors in a large oval around the small clearing, using the adjustable plastic straps to fix the devices to suitable pine trees surrounding the site.

"Okay, let's record some footage. Tom and Jessica, can you come over here? Alicia will make sure you both look good. It's just a few straightforward questions for the intro," Armstrong said, thrusting a laminated A4 card with a set of questions which had pre-typed responses on it, briefly detailing the events of the night before. "Are you happy with what's written on the sheets?" he asked them.

Tom studied the questions and responses. There wasn't anything too controversial, just details of their journey, time and details of where they'd set up camp, what they'd seen etc., stuff they'd discussed the evening before.

"No, all looks okay," Tom said, shrugging at Jess, who nodded her agreement.

"Okay, good. If you guys can stand over here, we'll capture the clearing and the top of the volcano rising from the pine forest. It looks perfect," Armstrong said.

Tom and Jess did as instructed.

"Let's roll," Armstrong shouted, to Doug and John who were already behind the cameras.

Armstrong then moved across them and in front of the camera being managed by John. "This is Richard Armstrong bringing you one of the most exciting editions of, 'The Planets Greatest Mysteries', directly on location in the pine forests of Mount Shasta, in the Cascade Mountain Range here in Siskiyou County, California, USA."

Armstrong then took Tom and Jess through the questions on the sheet whilst the two cameras rolled. Five minutes later they were done.

"That wasn't too bad was it? You both did well," Armstrong said, nodding at Alicia. "We'll edit the entire thing back in the U.K. and you can see the final version before we sign it off," he added.

"Fine," Tom said, nodding at Jess.

"Okay, let's get our tent pods set up, then we can relax a little, plan the next forty-eight hours that we have up here," Casey shouted from where he was standing by his vehicle.

Forty minutes later, Casey and Arran had set up two robust-looking four-man tent pods, complete with plastic windows and hard plastic doors. They looked almost solid, certainly less flimsy than the tents he and Jess had slept in the night before, but by no means good enough protection against that thing if it decided to return.

"What about you guys?" Casey shouted over to Armstrong, as he slotted the final door into a set of solid plastic-moulded hinges.

"Our accommodation is courtesy of Channel Five. Luxury bunk beds and goose feather quilts in the back of these mothers," Armstrong replied, patting the Merc's hood.

"You think we'd be staying in tents with that bloody Bigfoot roaming around?" Alicia said, grinning.

"Okay, okay, enough idle chit chat," Casey said, let's get dinner on the go. I'm sure everyone's hungry," he added.

It was approaching 6 p.m. by the time they were all seated around the fire, which was now glowing brightly in the middle of the clearing, crackling and popping as the wood burnt.

Tom sensed a growing feeling of Deja Vu from the evening before, which he pushed to the back of his mind.

Thirty minutes later, and Alicia started serving everyone some thick, vegetable stew, which she'd been cooking.

"I never knew about your hidden talents," Armstrong said, spooning some of the stew into his mouth.

"Yeah well there's lots you don't know about me. I used to live on a farm remember. My sisters and I often cooked our 'Grampa Johns' stew. Good isn't it?" she said, smugly.

"Fills a hole," Bruce said, smiling, a white cable trailing from one of his ears, the other end of which was plugged into a shoe-box sized device by his side. A large aerial extended out at a forty-five degree angle from it.

"Don't you ever stop eavesdropping," Alicia retorted.

"Someone has to do it."

Alicia forced a smile and raised her middle finger at him.

"So, I know it's not easy for you guys, but can you tell us again exactly what happened two nights ago up here?" Armstrong asked, clicking his fingers at John, who grabbed his handheld video camera from by his side in response.

Tom cleared his throat, and started recounting the events once again. He knew that this time it was for the benefit of the documentary however, so he was careful not to embellish the story in any way, not that he needed to.

"So I understand that you're a budding physicist and your passion lies in the search for extra-solar planets. What inspired you along this path?" Armstrong asked, in semi-interview mode.

Tom took a breath and looked up to the darkening sky. A few pinpricks of light were already visible in the heavens. "Well, my inspiration came from Carl Sagan. He's my hero. It's a shame he died when I was just a ten-year-old kid, but by then I was already hooked on his *Cosmos* TV series in the U.K. One of his quotes pretty much sums up how I feel; *'The universe is a pretty big place. If it's just us, it's an awful waste of space.'*

"Cut; cut! Excellent, excellent," Armstrong said, giving Tom the thumbs up sign.

There was a short silence as everyone appeared to stop and think about what Tom, or rather Carl Sagan had said. Only the crackle of the campfire as it popped and spat embers of burning wood permeated the clearing.

Just as Armstrong was about to speak, a hollow *thud...thud...thud* sound, as if someone were hitting a large tree with a baseball bat, echoed from somewhere deep in the forest, the source of the sound difficult to determine.

"What the hell was that?" Alicia asked, somewhat alarmed.

"Hopefully, just an overgrown, hungry woodpecker," Bruce shrugged, looking at the others, trying to make light of the noise.

Armstrong surveyed the darkening pine forest. "I was just about to say that I don't mind keeping first watch."

"That's fine by me. It's been a long day," Casey said, using a small sharp twig to pick something from between his teeth.

As they started to clear up, Jess turned to Tom. "What was that noise?"

Tom shook his head. "It could be anything. Maybe the military are closer than we think," he said. He was actually thinking back to a documentary he'd seen in the U.K. about Bigfoot hunters. The documentary had shown footage of supposed recordings of what was purportedly the sound of a Bigfoot communicating by using logs to bash against the sides of forest trees. He'd laughed at the suggestion at the time, but now his unease was growing.

The time was approaching midnight, and Tom and Jess were bedded down in their tent pod. Jess had just checked through the tent pod window for the third time to make sure Armstrong hadn't fallen asleep while on lookout; he hadn't.

"I feel a little safer now I must say," she whispered, snuggling up to Tom.

"Good, well we should be fine. I know that creature was big but it can't harm us with these guys around."

Tom's phone suddenly vibrated on the small plastic night table beside the bed, making him jump. He rolled his eyes and reached over to check the screen. A text message had come in from Gerry over at MIT.

Tom unlocked the phone using his thumb-print and read the message;

HI TOM, HOPE YOU'RE SAFE. JUST THOUGHT YOU'D WANT TO KNOW THAT THE UNITED NATIONS ARE MEETING TOMORROW IN N.Y. TO DISCUSS THE SIGNAL. THE EVENT WILL BE STREAMED LIVE, SO TRY TO BE CLOSE TO A LAPTOP AT 3 P.M. EASTERN TIME. I'VE ALSO DONE A BIT OF HACKING INTO NASA'S OFF-SITE FILES AND YOU'RE NOT GOING TO BELIEVE WHAT I'VE DISCOVERED. IT LOOKS LIKE A RETURN MISSION TO THE MOON IS BEING PREPARED, USING A HIGHLY CLASSIFIED, RECENTLY DEVELOPED, ADVANCED SPACECRAFT. THE MISSION HAS BEEN GIVEN THE CODENAME; ODYSSEY, AND IS SCHEDULED TO LAUNCH AT 20.00, PACIFIC TIME TOMORROW NIGHT!"

Four and a half miles northeast of their camp-site, a large, black, ten-wheeled truck was waved through the military checkpoint. Emblazoned on the truck's side was the SETI symbol; the words spelt with an upside down S, cleverly made to look like a question mark, and set inside a large radio dish, meant to represent the Arecibo – the world's second largest radio telescope in Arecibo, Puerto Rico and used by SETI to search for signals from space. The truck growled on up the mountain road, followed by two smaller white and green camouflage-painted military vehicles.

Inside the truck, Dr Lucy Davies and Professor Frederick Beck were seated around a small table, effectively what was a small mobile science laboratory in the rear of the large vehicle. A large monitor was fixed to the solid steel wall behind the driving cabin. The mystery signal was clearly displayed on the screen in a linear graph, its source only 3.8 miles distant, and a glacial region of Mount Shasta known as Cobalt Ridge.

Sitting opposite the SETI scientists was Lieutenant Coffey Jordan, a U.S. Military and Homeland Security Advisor, appointed to monitor the unfolding situation.

"Do we really need the military entourage? I mean, we're here to investigate the source of a radio signal, not an alien invasion," Dr Lucy Davies commented.

Jordan looked over at her. "They're here for your safety. We've no idea what we are dealing with and besides, two people have already gone missing up here in the last forty-eight hours, presumed dead. We don't want the contact team of what might well be the greatest ever scientific discovery, being attacked by a rogue grizzly bear or a goddamn Sasquatch, now do we."

Lucy sighed. "I still think it's over the top."

Before Jordan could respond, the three of them were distracted by the glow coming from the monitor. What had been a small red dot on the screen was now pulsating brightly and was increasing in intensity as they neared the glacial region of Cobalt Ridge.

"Come on, let's get ready," Jordan said, his expression serious and deadpan.

CHAPTER 13

A LOW, PULSATING alarm sounded somewhere outside the tent pod, waking Tom up with a start. He opened his eyes, trying to get his bearings for a moment, realising he must have drifted off to sleep some time ago. The siren seemed muffled at first, but quickly became clear. Someone, or something had set off the perimeter sensors.

He turned to wake Jess, but he didn't need to. She was already sat bolt upright in her sleeping bag, the sound striking a chord of fear into her. "What the hell is that?" she whispered.

"I don't know," Tom replied, grabbing his fleece jacket and pulling it on over his T-shirt. The alarm stopped momentarily but started sounding again. Tom cupped his hands against the pod's small plastic window and looked through it. Thirty feet away, a glowing computer screen where Armstrong had been keeping watch caught his attention. He then saw movement outside; it was Casey and Arran rushing over towards the glowing monitor.

"Stay here, you're completely safe. The guys are outside; I'll go and see what's going on. I'll be back shortly," he said to Jessica, as he quickly pulled his walking boots on over his thermal leggings.

Tom exited the pod and rushed over to where the guys were huddled over the screen, the perimeter breach alarm was still sounding.

"What's going on?" he asked, in a raised voice, just as the alarm fell silent again.

"We've got multiple breaches of the perimeter. One over on the northeast side and a breach directly ahead," Casey said, pointing towards the dark tree line.

Armstrong was already standing, his automatic rifle trained at the tree line. Tom strained his eyes, following the line of the rifle.

"Here, take these," Casey said, offering them each what appeared to be a set of night vision goggles he'd just pulled from a large canvas bag.

Tom grabbed them and pulled them on, Casey and Armstrong did likewise.

As Tom's eyes adjusted to the green backdrop, he noticed something large, dark, moving quickly just beyond the tree line. Whatever it was, it suddenly stopped. As it did, Tom was able to focus on the dark shape. It was large and as he watched it, the thing rose up on its two hind legs, its long, canine teeth appearing as a glistening, bright green-white colour through the goggles.

"Jeez, it's just a bear," Tom whispered in relief.

"It sure is a big mother," Casey said, as he directed his gaze to the same spot of forest.

Armstrong's two cameramen emerged from the dark Mercedes van parked a short distance behind them and walked over, bringing with them one of the film cameras. "What's up?" John asked.

"Perimeter alarm was triggered. Looks like one of the sensors was tripped by a bear," Armstrong said, lowering the gun to talk to the boys.

Suddenly, the alarm sounded again, indicating another perimeter breach had occurred. The monitor showed a second red blob at a location some fifty feet farther along from where the bear was positioned.

Tom swivelled his neck to focus on the spot. Moving quickly, ten feet deep beyond the tree line, were not one, but two large creatures. At first he thought they were more bears, even gorillas. They looked similar, but they were larger.

"Je – sus," Casey said, as he also spotted them. "Bigfoot, two of them," he uttered, in semi-disbelief.

"I hope you're filming all this," Armstrong said, staring at the events unfolding at the tree line. "Have you boys got the night lens on?"

"Of course boss," John said, directing the camera to where the men were looking. "What the hell?" he said, as the picked up the creatures closing in on the bear.

Tom watched in disbelief as the saw the two creatures appear to stalk the bear, which was still standing on its hind legs, presumably attempting to defend itself against the incoming, unknown threat.

The two Bigfoot moved quickly, one along the tree line, the other disappearing deeper into the pine forest as they closed in on the bear.

Thirty seconds later, the creatures attacked, one from the tree line, the other emerging from the depths of the forest, almost like a shark coming up from below. The bear let out a blood-curdling roar as it tried to defend itself against the creatures. One of the Bigfoot appeared to be carrying some kind of long tool that glinted in the moonlight as the creatures started smashing the bear like a pair of thugs beating a helpless kid with a baseball bat. The bear squealed as it tried to escape, but it had no chance. One of the creatures was now on the bear's back strangling it, punching its head with its huge, muscular gorilla-like arms. Then, with a sickening *crack* that was audible from where they were standing, the Bigfoot broke the bear's neck. The large brown bear became limp and fell to the ground.

"Jesus Christ, did you get all that?" Armstrong asked the camera guys.

"I...I think so," John stuttered back.

The men all watched in stunned silence through the night vision goggles as the creatures then started to drag the bear deeper into the forest. As Tom stared at the unfolding spectacle, one of the creatures stopped and looked back into the clearing, and then directly at them. A column of ice raced down Tom's spine as the thing appeared to stare at them momentarily, as if warning them not to follow, before it rejoined its mate, who was pulling the bear deeper into the forest and out of sight.

"That was freaking unbelievable!" Arran said, lowering his goggles.

Casey shook his head. "Seeing one Bigfoot, maybe I thought there was a chance, but seeing two attacking a bear. Never in my wildest dreams did I ever think I'd live to see that," he added.

"Having just one of us stand guard is clearly not an option. What if there are more than two of them? Three, maybe four? We might be out of our depth here," Armstrong said, clearly rattled at what he'd seen.

Tom heard Jess' voice and he spun around. "What's going on? I thought you were coming back to the pod."

"You'd better take Jessica back to the pod. We'll stay up and keep watch. You lot go get some rest. Arran and I will keep watch until dawn," Casey said, as he pulled out a box of ammunition from the canvas bag.

"Is everything all right?" Jess asked, anxiously.

"Come on. It's still only four a.m. Let's get back to bed. It was a false alarm," Tom said, as he led Jessica back towards their pod.

"Be out here for breakfast at seven a.m. sharp for a debriefing" Casey added.

Tom walked Jessica back to the pod, still trying to process what he'd just witnessed. He'd wait till the morning to tell Jess. There was no reason to scare the hell out of her now. He needed some more sleep to face what tomorrow might bring.

Three hours later, after a restless two and bit hours of sleep, Tom woke Jess to tell her what had happened during the early hours of the morning. He couldn't keep it from her any longer. She sat there, slowly shaking her head in stunned silence. "I just knew that it was a stupid reckless idea to come back here," she finally said.

"Look, I know it's bloody weird and scary, and we both knew deep down that it wasn't just a bear that attacked us back at the camp site. What I saw earlier verifies that. This entire thing is just unreal; the signal, everything that's going on here. But just think about it. We have two guys with high-powered automatic weapons. There's no way the creatures will attack us once those weapons are fired. I'm convinced we're pretty safe. I wouldn't risk our lives on this and besides, we owe it to Conner and Madison to do this. Try to find out what the hell is going on and where those things come from?" he said.

Jessica dropped her head. "I guess so," she muttered, after reflecting for a moment.

Jessica gave Tom a long hug and the pair of them joined the others outside who were all seated around where the fire had been burning the night before. A much smaller fire was now warming a pot of water to make some tea and coffee. A pot of beans was also warming alongside the tin kettle. Casey and Arran were chatting together, still gripping their weapons; clearly neither of them had yet been to bed.

"Morning. Did you tell Jess what happened last night?" Casey asked.

Tom nodded. "Yep of course; she's ok."

Casey nodded. "Good. Listen, we'll have some breakfast and then go and scout the perimeter, check the sensors and see if we can find anything. Then we will all walk to the signal site. It's only about a mile or so due northeast from here. We'll get back to this spot by mid-afternoon and set off before nightfall. How's that sound? Dickie can finish shooting his documentary and we can all return with the knowledge that Bigfoot isn't just a figment of people's imagination. We have definite proof of that now. What we have on film will astound the scientific world that's for sure. We will be safe tonight, out of the forest."

Everyone looked relieved.

"I'm happy with that. Okay with you guys?" Armstrong said, looking at his team for agreement.

"Bloody right boss. After watching what happened last night, I'm happy to get the hell off this weird mountain," Alicia said, stirring the pot of beans.

"Okay good. We're all in agreement then. What we already have on film will be worth a small fortune. Large bonuses for you all, I promise," Armstrong said, patting one of the cameras.

"Better be!" Alicia said, as they all finished breakfast.

The coffee tasted good, and Tom suddenly felt awake again. His mind was spinning as he tried to grasp what he'd seen last night, whilst wrestling with the bigger mystery of the signal that had been detected by SETI.

"Okay, Arran, you stay here and guard the camp, Dickie, John, and Tom will come with me and go take a look at the perimeter," Casey said, looking out through a set of binoculars at the tree line, some fifty feet distant.

Aaron nodded. "Go for it, Pa. We'll be fine here," he said.

"Don't venture too far," Jess said to Tom, as he stood up.

"It'll be fine. I very much doubt those things are around during the day," Tom said.

The four of them walked slowly to the tree line, John holding a large movie camera which he carried on his shoulder, filming everything as they proceeded into the pine forest.

"This looks like the spot where the attack took place," Casey said, pointing to the ground as they reached a point around ten feet in. On the forest floor was what appeared to be a dark patch of earth. A little farther along, they came across a blood-soaked fallen tree trunk. A layer of pine needles on the ground close by were also coated in blood.

"Okay, let's keep our wits about us and our eyes peeled. I'm sure those things are long gone, but let's just be careful," Casey said, as they proceeded deeper into the forest, following a bloodied, four-foot wide trail that had left by the dying, bear as it had been dragged deeper into the forest.

Around thirty feet into the forest, the bloody scuff marks appeared to end at a fallen tree. As the four of them negotiated the obstacle, Tom spotted something on the forest floor a short distance away. A low hum was also evident, flies swarming on what appeared to be one of the bear's severed arms, ripped clean from its body.

"Jeez, those things are damn strong to have done that," Casey said, his eyes darting between the dismembered arm and the dense forest surrounding them.

Armstrong turned to John. "Okay, let's get some footage. I'll introduce the scene, then you pan down to the severed arm," he whispered, nervously.

Armstrong started talking, as John filmed, confirming what they'd all seen last night and their current location on the mountain.

Tom surveyed the surrounding forest, he was feeling uneasy despite the weapons they had with them. He felt as if they were being watched. As Armstrong continued talking into the camera, Tom noticed a shaft of sunlight penetrating the tree canopy from above, which was reflecting off something lying on the forest floor, some fifteen feet away. The object appeared to be metallic, and was long and narrow.

Tom raised the binoculars to his face to get a better look. *That's curious*, he thought, as he stared at the object.

"What's up?" Casey's voice made him jump.

"There's something on the ground over there. Looks very odd," Tom said, pointing.

Tom and Casey made their way over to the object, which was half buried under foliage, pine needles, and creepers. It looked completely out of place lying on the forest floor.

"What the hell is it?" Casey asked, looking down.

Tom knelt and brushed away some of the pine needles. The object was about the length of a harpoon gun, similar in appearance, save for the fact there was no actual harpoon attached to it. It was constructed from a curious material, metallic, like tungsten. Tom touched what looked like the handle end. It felt cool and almost soft to the touch, like a hard gel. It felt very strange.

He pulled it from the foliage. The object felt lighter than its size would suggest, as if it were made from wood, not metal. And another odd quality, Tom realised, was that at some angles the object appeared to be translucent. *Weird, very weird*, Tom thought, as a shiver ran down his spine.

"Military you think?" Casey said.

"I've really no idea. It looks like a harpoon gun, but not one from this time and place," Tom added, as he picked the object up off the ground.

"What are you talking about? You're saying it's from the future?" Casey said, grinning.

"Is everything all right?" Armstrong shouted over from the spot where the bear's arm lay.

"We're coming now. We've found something very odd. Get the camera rolling," Casey said, as they headed over.

Tom thought about Casey's comment as he hurried back towards the clearing, the handle end of the object feeling as if it were slowly moulding itself to his grip.

CHAPTER 14

NASA/PENTAGON JOINT EMERGENCY MEETING

September 19, 10 A.M.

THE LARGE WALL-MOUNTED monitor flickered momentarily, as telemetry poured down the screen, the latest data on the location of the mystery signal and its apparent termination point, the *Saha impact crater* on the far side of the Moon.

A second, large monitor displayed the data for the additional signal that had been detected, which had its source at the same location on the Moon, and its termination point or origin, it wasn't possible to verify as yet, in the region of an Earth-like planet in the constellation of Cassiopeia.

"Do you think there is anything, I mean anything, significant about the Moon location, Professor Beck," Major Joseph Grant asked, as he lit up a fat, Havana cigar.

Beck shook his head. "The region was mapped and photographed by the Soviet Union's *Luna Three* space probe, but of course we've never been there. I don't need to remind you the U.S. Government pulled the plug on the Saturn Vs in 1974 after the last Moon mission."

General Grant grunted. "Well, we figured there wasn't much else to find. We achieved our goal at the time by beating the Russians up there. Our next target is Mars, far more exciting – or so we thought." The general took a long pull on his cigar, and blew the smoke out over everyone's heads and sat in silence, as if deep in thought. "How long did it take our Saturn V's to reach the Moon, Professor?" he asked.

Frederick Beck shifted on his seat, and thought back to the Saturn V launches. "Around three days."

"Three days. A lot can happen in three days, but I suppose five decades ago that wasn't too bad," the general said, blowing out a large smoke ring, which drifted idly up towards the ceiling.

"What if I were to tell you we had a craft that could get three men to the Moon in less time than it takes to drive from Los Angeles to Las Vegas. Is that something that would interest you?"

Beck turned to Lucy and his other two SETI colleagues and then back at the general. "You're talking less than four hours?" he questioned.

"Probably less, but about right," the general said, expelling a plume of smoke from his never-ending cigar.

Beck shook his head. "That's impossible. Our New Horizons probe was the fastest craft ever to reach the moon. It passed it in eight and a half hours after launch, travelling at thirty-six thousand miles an hour on its way to Pluto. Are you saying you have something faster than that?"

"The general leaned back in his chair and stretched. I'm not saying anything. Your job is to assemble some suitable astronauts in the next twelve hours. Do that and we can get them to the Moon by six tomorrow evening."

The general leaned forward. "We need to get back up there ASAP to find out what the hell that signal is. Why it terminates on the Moon, and what is transmitting the second signal towards the constellation Cassiopeia. Just get me those astronauts,' gentlemen," he said, standing up.

The two military men walked to the door. "We will be in touch at ten p.m. to discuss this further. I'll expect some developments and suggestions as to what we do when we get to the location of the transmission. The astronauts also need to be de-briefed before we can allow them to go."

The two scientists just stared at the general and his sidekick as they left the room, their jaws hanging open in disbelief.

CHAPTER 15

Mount Shasta, 7.40 P.M.

THE SUN HAD just started to dip behind the pine trees leaving a distinct chill filling the air as Casey struck a match to light the tinder under the pile of wood he'd assembled.

"Have you figured out what that thing is yet?" he asked Tom, raising his voice above the sound of the crackling wood.

Tom shook his head. "No idea. It looks like a weapon of some kind, but you've studied it, there are no buttons or trigger on it that I can see. I've taken a photo and sent it on to Gerry over at MIT He might come up with something," Tom said.

Alicia, Armstrong, and Arron were grouped together a short distance away, at the edge of the pine forest. Armstrong wanted some atmospheric footage for the documentary, having earlier filmed and speculated with the group over what the mystery harpoon-like object might be. It was all perfect material for the documentary.

Bruce was on his computer doing some research on the mountain, specifically the old mineshafts dotted around the area. "Hmm, this is interesting," he said, looking up from his laptop. "According to this article, some of these mineshafts extend right up under the mountain. Could be a good addition to the documentary if nothing else," he said, half to himself.

Tom turned his head to study the tin shack at the edge of the clearing they'd passed yesterday. He'd forgotten about it after the excitement of finding the strange object in the forest. "Well, let's go check it out," he said, carefully placing the harpoon-like object on a towel he'd laid on the grass. "You coming?" he asked Jessica.

"Yeah, I guess," she said, getting up.

Tom grabbed the small flashlight, and he and Jess wandered over to the edge of forest near to the narrow track they'd driven up yesterday. The light was beginning to fade, and the forest was looking dark and unsettling either side of the route.

The shack was a simple construction, made from corrugated steel sheeting that formed the roof and sides, which was riveted over thick wood and steel beams. The entire thing was built against the side of what looked like a solid area of rock that protruded up from the ground. The sides and roof were now covered in vines and undergrowth, concealing the entire construction quite nicely. There was no door, just a dark void that disappeared into the mine shaft.

"I'm not bloody going in there," Jessica protested as they reached the shack.

"Hmm, it looks a bit creepy, I grant you," Tom said.

"Looks like the entrance to the Ghost Train ride, but worse," she said.

"Stay there, I just want to take a look inside. Don't worry, I'm not going into the mineshaft," Tom said, turning the flashlight on.

Tom entered the shack, which was around eight feet square and panned the interior with the flashlight. Over in the far right corner he saw a wooden table, on top of which sat two old lanterns and an old, rusty tin. A few oily rags hung from rusted hooks on the opposite corner.

Directly ahead, Tom could see the mineshaft, hewn from solid rock, which descended and disappeared off to the left at a gentle angle in the direction of the mountain. There were ancient, rusted hand rails bolted to the sides of the shaft, and a well-worn narrow gauge track embedded in the ground, leading into the mine. Tom shone the flashlight into the dark tunnel, the beam of light from his torch casting weird shadows against the tunnel walls, created by the jagged, rough rock. He was just about to turn and leave when the beam of light washed over something on the ground, just where the tunnel bent to the left. "There's something in the tunnel, Jess, just a short distance away. I'm going to go in and take a look," Tom said, turning towards Jess whose grey, shadowy figure was barely visible standing just outside the entrance to the mine.

Tom carefully walked the twenty-five feet to reach the object, which appeared to be an old wooden casket the size of a cooler box. He reached down and grabbed the side handles, which creaked as he pulled on them. As he did, he felt his wrist brush against a thick, spider's web. He yanked the casket up off the ground and walked briskly towards the light, where Jessica was waiting for him. Tom emerged from the dark tunnel and dropped the weighty casket onto the ground just outside the shack. As he did, Jessica screamed.

"Jesus Christ, Tom, you've got a freaking massive spider on your shoulder."

Tom didn't see himself as squeamish, but didn't like the thought of a spider being anywhere near him either. Especially one he couldn't see. He shrieked in response to Jess' comment and jumped up and down in an attempt to shake the critter off him. Tom felt what could only have been one of the spider's legs tickle his neck. He freaked out, yanked his jumper and T-Shirt off, and started cursing.

Bruce and Doug came running over from the fire. "What the hell is going on?" Bruce shouted.

"Tom went into the mine and came out with a bloody huge spider on his shoulder," Jess shrieked.

"Calm down, buddy. There's nothing on you now," Doug said, reassuring Tom.

Tom's jumper was lying on the ground a short distance away. As Tom went to retrieve it, a saucer-sized black spider scuttled off into the undergrowth.

The four of them watched it leave. "Hmm, I think you'd have been ok," Bruce shrugged. "That was a Lampshade spider. It looks gruesome, but is fairly harmless!"

"Come face to face with a Bigfoot but freak out over a spider!" Arran, who'd come over to see what was going on, teased.

Tom shook his head and took in a deep breath of air. "Stop arsing around and help me with this chest; let's take it over to the camp," he said, grabbing his shirt and jumper from the ground.

Bruce grabbed one end of the casket, Tom the other and they walked it over to the camp-fire.

Armstrong and his film crew were just heading back from filming a scene at the edge of the forest. "What have you found?" he asked Tom, intrigued.

"A casket of some kind. It was in the old mineshaft. I'm just about to open it," Tom said.

"Okay hold on, let's film it being opened," Armstrong said, clicking his fingers at John.

Tom waited for John to run over with the camera to start filming, before flipping up the heavy central clasp that was holding the lid of the casket in place.

Tom lifted the lid, which creaked open.

"It's empty?" Armstrong bellowed, disappointed.

"Not quite. There's something here," Tom said, pulling out an old, worn yellow piece of parchment that wasn't immediately visible.

"Oh, wow, it's a treasure map!" Alicia said, suddenly interested.

Tom carefully opened the piece of parchment which had been folded into eight sections.

"It's definitely some kind of map," he said.

"Are you serious?" Alicia said, glancing over Tom's shoulder to get a better look.

With the parchment unfolded and laid out on the ground, the group could see what was clearly a drawing of Mount Shasta marked in faded ink. Leading inwards were numerous routes, presumably the mineshafts that were dotted around the area. One of the routes on the map ended in what appeared to be a large, underground cavern. The scale on the map suggested it was around half a mile from their current location.

"That's very interesting," Bruce said, bringing his laptop over and comparing the image he had on screen with the unfolded piece of parchment. On the laptop screen was a similar plan of the mine system. It showed more or less the same routes. The only thing that was different was on the actual parchment, which showed the cavern feature.

"Check this out," Bruce said, enthusiastically. "See this shaft here. It meets another shaft a hundred feet along, which seems to lead to this cavern feature on the parchment. He paused before speaking again. "You know what I'm thinking?"

Tom was thinking the same thing, but surely it would be too coincidental?

"You're not thinking this cavern area could be close to where the signal is emanating from?" Tom suggested.

"Well it has to be pretty close. We have the coordinates. Check this out," Bruce said, as he punched the keyboard. "I've overlaid the signal source graphic onto the map of the tunnels and look," he said, pointing.

Tom studied the screen. He found their current location, indicated by a blue dot that Bruce had cleverly overlaid onto the map using the I-Pad's satellite app. The mineshaft behind them was visible, as was another longer shaft that intersected it, and continued on to the cavern shown on the old parchment.

"Okay that's enough for now," Armstrong said, to John who'd been filming since Tom opened the casket.

The fire popped behind them, just as an owl hooted from somewhere deep in the forest.

"Oh god that signals the day is drawing to a close again. After tonight, I'm done, Tom. I really don't think I can spend another night on this damn mountain," Jess said.

"You and I both, honey. Don't worry; I'll insist we leave tomorrow as planned." Tom wasn't going to break his promise but there was no way he was going to be leaving without first checking out the cavern shown on the map, especially if it was close to the location of the mystery signal SETI had detected.

"Okay who's up for some hot dogs?" Alicia shouted over from the fire.

"Ah, perfect timing. I'll crack open some Merlot," Armstrong said, heading over to one of the trucks.

Tom and Jess walked over to the fire and each grabbed a hotdog from Alicia. As they all sat eating around the fire, Armstrong asked, "So, guys, I know it's tempting to check the mineshaft out, but my preference is to head to the signal area overland. The film crew have no option. We're not insured for any underground filming, and those shafts are ancient. There's no way we can guarantee anyone's safety."

Jess rolled her eyes. "Some common sense at last!" she said.

"If we leave for Cobalt Ridge at first light, we can be back in town before dark. How's that?"

"Thank god for that," Jessica replied.

Embers popped from the fire and landed on Alicia's knee.

"Shit!" she screamed, quickly brushing them off.

As silence descended once again, Tom felt his phone vibrate in his pocket. He pulled it out. There was a message waiting from Gerry over at MIT. He opened it up and slowly read the text, then read it again to make sure he'd digested it correctly.

I CARRIED OUT A SEARCH UNDER VARIOUS PHRASES 'PERSONAL WEAPON', 'UNUSUAL WEAPON', 'ANCIENT WEAPON', AND 'ADVANCED WEAPON', UNDER THE CATEGORIES OF 'SPEAR', 'SWORD', AND 'GUN', IN ALL THE USUAL DATA BASES, BOTH ACTUAL, MYTHOLOGICAL AND LEGENDARY AND THIS IS THE CLOSEST MATCH - THE PREFERRED WEAPON OF NINURTA WHO IS THE SUMERIAN AND AKKADIAN HERO-

GOD OF WAR AND HUNTING. MAKES NO SENSE TO ME, BUT IT'S WHAT
THE SYSTEM IS THROWING BACK AT ME.

Tom frowned. It had to be an error. What on earth would an
ancient mythological weapon be doing lying on the ground in
Mount Shasta's Trinity National Park? Nothing made sense.

"That a message from Gerry?" Casey asked.

Tom slowly nodded his head. "Yep, but you're not going to
believe what it says."

CHAPTER 16

CASEY THREW MORE thick branches onto the fire to keep it going, the flames quickly starting to dance higher in response.

Tom had spent the last hour hunched over the laptop, searching for any relevant information on *Ninurta* and links to the Sumerians and the Weapon of Legend, however there wasn't much else to be found. He stretched and was about to close the laptop when a low, distant rumble, more of a growl, emanated from the forest, somewhere off to their right, on the eastern side.

"What the hell was that?" Casey said, leaving the fire and grabbing his rifle, which was standing up against one of the camera tripods. He raised it to his shoulder in order to use the night vision scope to scan the dark forest.

"Oh Jesus, those creatures are coming back to get us," Jess said.

"Well, we are at the base an active volcano. It could be some seismic activity. Maybe Shasta's waking up?" Tom suggested.

"I bloody hope not. I can't see anything," Casey called out, as he continued panning the eastern edge of the forest.

The sound briefly drifted out of the forest again, carried on the evening breeze.

"I don't like this one bit," Casey said, as Armstrong grabbed a set of night vision goggles from the small table and joined him, while he continued panning the forest with the night vision scope on his rifle.

"Something's not right. It doesn't sound like seismic activity. Come on, let's get our backpacks," Tom whispered to

Jess," as he grabbed the object they'd found in the forest and ran with her to their tent pod. They quickly packed the few items they had into their backpacks before re-joining the team, who were all standing nervously by the crackling fire, which was the only sound that could now be heard.

"I think I just saw something," Casey said, nodding his head towards an area of forest over to the right.

Armstrong, who still had the night vision goggles pressed to his face, panned over to the location.

"Shit!" he suddenly spat out, after a few short seconds. "You're right, we've got company."

"We sure have, but not the sort we want. It's the military," Casey growled.

Armstrong turned to Tom and shouted. "There's no time. I know you want to explore the mines, and now's your chance. Take the small video camera and go!"

"I'm coming with you," Bruce said, folding his laptop and stuffing it in its carrier case.

"Well you're not going to leave me alone!" Jess said, looking at Tom.

"Of course not, let's go, quick!" Tom agreed, holding out his hand.

Jess grabbed Tom's hand, and the three of them sprinted for the entrance to the mineshaft, just as a vehicle's bright neon headlights punched through the edge of the forest, followed by the sound of its powerful engine.

Tom turned on the flashlight as the three of them ran into the mineshaft. From the clearing outside, a mechanical, amplified voice echoed into the shaft. "This is the United States Military. Put down your weapons and stand still or you will be shot."

The three of them continued around the left hand bend of the shaft where Tom had found the chest earlier. The beam of light from the torch bounced off the walls and roof of the mine as they ran, revealing thick, wooden support beams covered in lichen and cobwebs. After a minute, and with the immediate threat of the military finding them receding, the three of them stopped, panting rapidly to catch their breath.

"Jesus Christ that was close. What a total disaster," Tom gasped, brushing a cobweb from his forehead.

"We're going to end up in serious trouble if we get caught now," Jessica whispered between breaths.

"Well, we don't plan on doing that now, do we?" Bruce replied, rolling his eyes.

"Come on; let's continue as we can't go back now. I'm sure Armstrong will think of something to say to get out of the crap they're in. The mystery signal and all the other weird stuff going on here is too important to ignore. There's a cover-up I'm sure, especially as the military are involved," Tom said.

"Damn right there. It's like one of those old sci-fi B movies from the 1950s. *The Day the Earth Stood Still*, or *The Blob*," Bruce said.

"That was a classic. Steve McQueen, before he was a movie star," Tom replied.

"Yeah that's right."

"I loved *Them*," Tom's voice echoed along the mineshaft.

"*Them*, Damn I'd forgotten about that movie; giant ants take over L.A right? That was a classic."

"Can you guys shut the hell up? I'm scared shitless as it is without you two talking about stupid sci-fi movies," Jessica interrupted.

"Sorry Jess. Here, you can do some filming of your own," Tom said, handing Bruce the movie camera.

The three of them continued along the mine, Tom's flashlight casting eerie shadows as the beam of light swept the shaft ahead of them, bouncing off the solid rock walls and timber roof beams used to strengthen the mineshaft.

The air temperature was becoming noticeably colder as they proceeded deeper into the mine and moved towards the glacial area at the base of Mount Shasta.

Two miles northwest of their location, the black SETI truck, accompanied by two military Humvees, pulled off the main mountain road onto a snow-covered track, which lay above the tree line, just beneath Mount Shasta's eastern face. An old weathered, wooden sign, leaning at a jaunty angle pointed the way to *Cobalt Ridge Glacier*, the apparent source of the mystery signal.

Inside the vehicle, Dr Lucy Davies stared at the monitor and the glowing blue dot, which was hovering over a location just 600 feet away from their current position.

"I can't believe this is actually happening. I mean the signal, it has to be genuine. The data can't be wrong," Lucy gushed, her heart starting to race with excitement.

The truck rumbled on, its spiked, winter ice tyres gripping into the narrow icy track, which was becoming increasingly treacherous the higher up the eastern side of the volcano they drove.

"So what do you guys figure this signal really is? I mean, if it's genuine, surely we need to be concerned about it?" Jordan asked.

Lucy didn't respond to Jordan's question for a few seconds, still engrossed in the readings on the monitor in front of her, making him repeat the question.

"Oh, sorry, well that's a reasonable question. Yes and no," Lucy replied. "I mean, if the signal is genuine and actually comes from an alien civilisation, then it's truly the most significant scientific discovery we could ever make. It could change everything. Our understanding of our place in the universe, humankind's origins, and who we really are as a species, perhaps even who created us. I mean the ramifications of this are mind-boggling," she said, tearing her eyes away from the glowing blue dot on the monitor for a few seconds.

"What if whoever is sending this signal has hostile intent?" Jordan asked.

"Well, to be frank that's highly unlikely. Any advanced intelligence could annihilate us in a second if it wanted to, probably without any warning, or us even realising it had happened," Professor Beck said.

"That's true. Any civilisation advanced enough to make contact indicates they are benevolent enough not to have destroyed themselves, or indeed to have any intention of destroying us."

"I'd prefer to trust my instinct on that theory. A signal that emanates from a glacier on earth, and terminates somewhere in the Cassiopeia Star System, via the Moon, either has to be a hoax, or something to be very wary of in my book," Jordan said.

"Why, that's your job isn't it, to be wary? That's why the U.S. Military is involved in all this. Trust nobody; be suspicious of everybody, and fingers on the trigger of whatever killing machines you possess, ready to blast anything you think is a threat to kingdom come. Let's face it, during the last fifty years its pure luck the United States and Russia haven't destroyed this planet many times over," Lucy said, with disdain.

Jordan said nothing.

The truck slowed and took a sharp right turn, climbing farther up the mountain pass.

"According to the monitor, we are now only two hundred feet away from the source," Lucy exclaimed, her eyes wide with excitement.

Jordan's radio sprang to life with a burst of static. "Yes sir, will do. Over and out," he said, after a short pause.

"Don't tell us. We won't be able to see the location until you guys have secured the area?" Lucy said.

"It's just a precaution and for your own safety ma'am. You need to stay in the truck until I advise you further."

The truck slowed, and after a minute came to a halt on a flat ridge of ice, at the edge of the tree line. The two Humvees that had been following pulled to a stop alongside, their powerful, diesel engines falling silent seconds later.

Lucy started to feel nervous as she glanced at the screen in front of her, the glowing blue dot right upon them. The ground-penetrating radar fitted to the SETI vehicle confirming the exact location of the signal was around thirty feet due west from their location and some fifteen feet beneath the glacial ice. The thought that the signal really could be alien in nature sent a shiver down her spine. She had to admit, it was a little odd the source was coming from under a glacial area of a mountain on the continental U.S.A. It made little sense.

Jordan grabbed his M14, checked the magazine to ensure it was loaded, and opened the back of the vehicle before jumping down to the ground. A freezing gust of air blew into the truck as he slammed the door shut again.

Lucy shivered and rubbed her arms in response to the sudden blast of cold air. "Come on, let's get kitted up," she said, finishing the dregs of the coffee she'd been drinking.

Professor Beck got up from the desk and grabbed the two parkas that were hanging in the corner, passed one to Lucy, then walked over to a cabinet and pulled out a portable, depth-penetrating radar device. "Have you considered what we're going to do if we can't get access to whatever is emitting the signal?"

Lucy zipped up her parka "Yep, we're going to melt our way down to it," she said, winking at him.

CHAPTER 17

JOINT NASA/SETI U.S. PRESIDENT BRIEFING
MEETING - OVAL OFFICE.

THE SEYMOUR TALL Case Clock standing against the wall of the Oval Office ticked to 11 p.m. Eastern Daylight Time as the small team of scientists and military officials were ushered into the Whitehouse's most important room, where President Trent was sat behind his desk, hands folded across his stomach. "Sit, gentlemen," he said to the men who'd just entered.

NASA Advanced Space Mission Science Director Dr Edgar Bond and SETI scientist Dr Hans Willems sat, the two military personnel also each took a chair.

"So, gentlemen, what's the latest position in this very unusual, and somewhat exciting, situation we find ourselves in? Should we be readying our nukes?" the president asked, smirking at General Joseph Grant as he spoke.

The general nodded and opened a small notebook he was holding. "Well, sir, our army recon unit, together with the SETI field scientists reached the remote glacial location, *Cobalt Ridge,* on the eastern flank of Mount Shasta an hour or so ago. The site is secure, and the source of the signal has been pinpointed to a location approximately fifteen feet beneath the ice. GPR has confirmed there is a sub-glacial cavern or hollow at the source point. SETI scientist, Dr Lucy Davies, who is on the ground there, has suggested melting through the glacier to get to whatever is emitting the signal, but we are looking at other possible entry points. Perhaps drilling into the ground and inserting a fibre optic camera in first, to see what we're dealing with, might be the safest option. It's low risk and will give us a good visual of what's going on. As for the nukes, I don't believe that's necessary just yet. We have suitable military assets in the area we can utilise, including a squadron of F-35's on standby at Beale Air Force Base should we need them."

The president nodded. I like that, clean, quick, and safe. I was joking about the nukes, but the F-35's are a good idea." he said, before turning to the NASA and SETI scientists. "What's the latest on the science side?"

SETI scientist, Dr Willems, a middle-aged, no-nonsense guy, took the end of the pencil he was chewing out of his mouth. "Yes, Mr. President, as the general said, the source of the signal lies fifteen feet beneath the Cobalt Ridge Glacier. At this point in time, we have no idea what technology is involved in the transmission. The logical conclusion was that it was man- made, but the second signal originating on the Moon and focused towards the constellation of the Cassiopeia star system does, of course, suggest otherwise."

The president narrowed his eyes and thought for a few seconds. "So, if it's not the Russians, the Chinese, or the dammed North Koreans, you're saying it might actually be alien in nature?"

Willems shrugged his shoulders. "As incredible as it seems, there's nothing else it could be."

The president took in a deep breath, before slowly exhaling. "What's the position with Operation Odyssey? Are we ready to launch the X40?"

NASA scientist, Dr Edgar Bond, according to his name badge, ran his hand through his mob of curly brown hair. "The craft is being fuelled as we speak. It takes thirty-six hours to fill her. The advanced plasma engines have been primed and we'll be ready to go in three hours from now; eleven p.m. Pacific Time. ETA on the Moon should be zero-two-thirty a.m. PT time, eleven-thirty p.m. EDT," he said.

"And the astronauts, are you satisfied they are up to the task?" President Trent asked, moving a glass paperweight prism around on his desk.

Bond nodded. "A little more time would have been nice, but they're good to go."

"Very well gentlemen. That's what I wanted to hear. As for *Cobalt Ridge*, we will get everything prepared for a vertical melt through the ice if we can't get the cameras into the cavern before we are on the Moon. I want to know what's going on beneath that glacier before our boys step foot on the Moon."

"Yes sir. Oh, there is one more thing," General Grant said.

The president raised his eyebrows.

"The military unit just came across a British film production company, two miles due south of the signal source. Claimed they were making a documentary about the alleged Bigfoot attack on four campers the other day. Two campers are still missing, presumed dead. One of the survivors is a Brit, Tom Bishop, a recent graduated from MIT with a first in Physics. He and his girlfriend are still on the mountain, as we found some heavy-duty sleeping pods."

The president shook his head. "This whole thing gets more bizarre each day. Needless to say I'll not be raising that at the UN meeting in just under an hour. I take it the group are being cleared off the mountain and taken in for questioning."

The general nodded. "As we speak."

"Very well, there's nothing else to say. Good day to you all and good luck. I need to deal with the gathering crowds outside the gates and brief the Russians and the Chinese of the situation ahead of the UN meeting. If this signal turns out to be what we think it is, we don't want any misunderstandings or confusion," President Trent affirmed.

CHAPTER 18

Mount Shasta Copper Mines, 8 P.M.

THE THREE OF them had been walking through the mineshaft for half an hour, with the temperature dropping noticeably as they travelled farther in. A damp, almost mouldy smell hung in the air. Jessica shivered as she walked, staying as close as she could to Tom. "I wonder what's happened to the others. It's just a matter of time before the army come after us you know. At least it will be the end of this crazy adventure when they do," she said, her voice echoing in the dark tunnel.

Tom checked his mobile phone. As expected, there was no signal, and no further messages from Gerry.

The mineshaft started to curve around to the right and appeared to be rising ever so slightly to the surface. The passage's rocky walls, blasted through the solid bedrock had more and more patches of green moss or lichen covering them. A distinct trickle of running water could be heard coming from somewhere up ahead, no doubt melting glacial ice from above. "Careful, it's becoming a bit slippery," Tom warned, as he felt his boots lose purchase on the ground.

The three of them continued on in silence for another forty feet, when Bruce suddenly froze in his tracks.

"What the hell?" he said, staring at Tom.

"What's up?" Tom asked, stopping as he saw the shocked look on Bruce's face. As he spoke, he realised what Bruce was referring to. An eerie, ultra-violet hue filled the tunnel, bathing the three of them, and the immediate space around them in a warm purple/blue glow.

"Jesus Christ," Tom shouted, discarding his backpack, together with the harpoon-like object, the source of the light. His backpack fell to the ground, the ultra violet light emanating from the device glowing brighter, bathing the tunnel twenty feet either side of them in an intense violet light.

"Are you okay?" Jess asked.

"Yep, fine, I didn't feel anything," Tom replied, aghast, as the three of them backed away from the backpack, shielding their eyes from the light as they did.

"Is it going to explode?" Jessica screamed, gripping Tom's hand as if it were a stress ball.

"I've no idea. It's fucking weird, man," Tom said, using language he rarely let slip past his lips. Before any of them had a chance to speak further, the glow coming from the object started to fade, until all that was left was a purple halo around the device, making it look like a cheap, child's toy.

"Is it safe?" Jess whispered.

"No idea, but it hasn't exploded," Tom replied, his voice barely audible. "Stay put. I'm going to have a closer look," he said.

Bruce remembered he was holding the video camera and quickly turned it on to start filming the strange event.

Tom crouched by his backpack, and shielding his eyes with one arm, in case it started glowing intensely again, placed his left hand over his backpack and the harpoon that was strapped to the outside. "It still feels a little warm," he whispered. He took a deep breath and quickly touched the handle end of the object with his finger. It felt okay, not hot.

Tom stared at the object as the ultra-violet glow continued to slowly fade until the glow was barely noticeable and the tunnel was in darkness again. "That was extraordinary," he whispered, realising that whatever the object was, it was beyond their current level of comprehension. Could it be some kind of top secret, U.S. Military advanced weapon or something even more sinister? He wondered. Surely they weren't looking at alien technology? He pushed the absurd thought to the back of his mind and reached out for his backpack. "Well, it doesn't appear to be a threat," he said, pulling the pack, along with the strange device, back onto his back.

"Come on, let's move on, and see if we can find the cavern shown on the old map. I've a feeling there might be more than just a pile of gold stashed there," he said.

"It's a good job I've got this video camera. Nobody would believe what just happened if I hadn't caught that on film," Bruce said.

"And that's a good thing?" Jessica added, as the three of them set off again along the tunnel.

five hundred feet behind them, out in the clearing in the pine forest, the major finished finger printing and scanning the retinas of Armstrong's film crew. Casey had already been cuffed and placed in the army Humvee for pissing the general off and was now under military detention, whatever that meant. Arran's protest had fallen on deaf ears and he'd had to bite his lip for fear of ending up in the same position as his father. Armstrong had told his team to say as little as possible, but to cooperate. He'd shown the general his credentials, U.S. visa, and Channel Five journalist pass, which, as he'd hoped, had afforded him and his team some latitude. At least the M14's had been lowered and they didn't feel under immediate threat any more.

"Right, my men will be driving your vehicles and equipment out of here and back to Alpha Base, where a military unit will meet us and take you back down into Shasta for debriefing. Do you understand?"

Armstrong nodded. "Come on, guys, let's do as the general asks," he said, winking at Alicia.

The general eyed them cautiously as they each got into the Humvee. As Armstrong pulled himself in, he noticed a flash of light deep in the pine forest. The sun's fading rays glinting off something shiny, he wondered, or were his eyes playing tricks on him? He was exhausted after all. He sat down next to Alicia and felt a jolt as the Humvee jerked out of a rut it had been parked in, and turned in a wide arc in the clearing to head back down the mountain track they'd travelled up earlier.

"You okay?" Armstrong asked Alicia, over the growl of the Humvee's powerful V8 diesel engine as it negotiated the narrow track out of the clearing.

"Yes, boss," she replied, rolling her eyes. "Wasn't banking on this shit though," she added.

"Me neither. I'm really sorry. We've enough incredible footage to cobble together an amazing documentary though."

"What if they confiscate our equipment? They're bound to after all."

"Don't worry, it's secure and already downloaded," Armstrong said, winking, just as the Humvee hit another rut, jostling them all in their seats. John and Doug were seated opposite and looked scared. They'd not said much since the military unit had emerged from the forest. "Don't worry boys. We'll be okay. They can't do much to us. We'll be on a flight back to the U.K. before you can say *Yeti*," Armstrong said, trying to make light of their situation.

"Ha, bloody ha," John replied, forcing a smile.

"Assholes," Arran muttered.

Armstrong looked out the small window into the darkening woods, wondering where Tom and the others were. Had they found the cavern shown on the map? As he looked into the forest, he thought he saw some movement, and caught a glimpse of a flash of light again. What the hell was it?

"Did you just see that?" he asked Alicia and the boys. "Outside; I just saw a flash of light. I saw the same thing as I got into the vehicle."

"No," Alicia said, craning her neck to look out the window.

The Humvee started to slow down. A crackled voice filtered through from the cabin. "… blocked. Fallen trees, manoeuvring around…"

Armstrong looked at Alicia. "Odd, we didn't have the same problem on the way up yesterday."

"Something's not right, boss, I'm scared," Alicia whispered.

The Humvee's engine changed pitch as it carefully turned off the track into the forest, and through a natural clearing in the pine trees, following the vehicle in front.

As they drove into the trees, Armstrong caught a glimpse of the huge Douglas-fir tree blocking the route, with its trunk literally snapped at the base, huge splinters of healthy tree clearly visible.

The lead vehicle drove in a wide arc, passing the fallen tree, before started to turn back towards the dirt track, slowly manoeuvring in between the large pine trees.

"We're heading back onto the track," Armstrong said, just as there was a loud *crack* from outside, followed by a *thud* as the Humvee in front literally vanished from view.

The vehicle they were travelling in jerked to a halt. "What the fuck?" one of the military guys in the front shouted.

Armstrong leant over Alicia to try to get a better look out the side window, but all he could see was a cloud of dust and the ends of what appeared to be tree trunks jutting out at various angles where the front Humvee had been moments earlier. The route down the mountain where the tree canopy wasn't so thick was still fairly light, but the forest either side was dark, the sun's fading rays unable to penetrate it.

"Okay, stay put you lot. We're going to find out what's going on," a voice ordered from the front cabin over the communication system. The two military guys got out, M14 Carbines gripped in their hands, and slowly walked towards where the Humvee had disappeared from sight.

The five of them could just about see what was going on through the side window, the vehicle's headlights lighting up the forest around them.

The two military men came to a stop, just fifteen feet ahead and appeared to be looking down into some kind of hole that had opened up. *Could it be some kind of mud slide, or sink hole?* Armstrong wondered. He'd heard a lot about sink holes on the news and was going to do a documentary on them. Holes that just opened up in the ground due to the collapse of the surface layer, swallowing whatever was on top. Buildings and even people's houses had been gobbled up by them.

Armstrong grabbed his binoculars and raised them to his face to take a closer look. He could instantly tell that this was no sinkhole. There were tree trunks and healthy pine tree branches, clearly recently torn from the surrounding trees, sticking out at various angles from what was clearly some kind of man-made, or at least purposely dug pit, which the Humvee had clearly fallen into.

"It's a trap. We need to get out of here," he said, putting the binoculars back in his jacket pocket. "It looks like the Humvee has fallen into a pit."

"You're kidding?" Alicia said, her hands shaking.

As Armstrong went to get out, one of the military men appeared at the door. "You stay put. We have an incident up ahead. We need to pass a rope down to our colleagues. Vehicle seems to have fallen into a sink hole," he growled.

The second military guy walked around to the back of the Humvee and disappeared from view, reappearing thirty seconds later with a thick length of rope over his shoulder. He moved to the front of the Humvee and knelt. Armstrong guessing he must be tethering one end of the rope to the front of the vehicle somewhere. Both men then proceeded back to the pit and threw the other end of the rope in.

Armstrong could see the men looked concerned, scanning the forest, their M14's levelled, as if ready to engage a target.

Within a minute or so, the four of them watched from the vehicle as the first man emerged from the pit. Armstrong grabbed his binoculars again and could see the man had a nasty and bloodied gash to his head. He was pointing into the forest, and then back down towards the pit. A second man climbed up, collapsing onto the ground as he tried to stand.

Suddenly, a brilliant flash of violet light lit up the dark forest over to their right. And then, as if they were staring in their own science fiction movie, a laser-like strip of light streaked out from the forest where the bright glow had been, striking the four military men who were standing at the edge of the pit. Armstrong and the other three watched in stunned silence as the men briefly glowed a bright purple-violet, before vanishing in a puff of dust, as if they had been vaporised.

"Oh Jesus, what the fuck is going on?" Alicia shrieked.

"Come on; let's get the hell out of here. Quick, run. Run, back to the campsite," Armstrong ordered.

CHAPTER 19

S4 GROOM LAKE BASE, AREA 51

Papoose Dry Lake, Nevada, 10 Miles South of Area 51
X40 Launch Control, 11 P.M.

MOONLIGHT BATHED THE mountain range separating Papoose Lake from the Groom Lake test facility in Lincoln County, Nevada. In the northeast corner, close to the base of the mountain ridge, a rattle snake slid out from a desert camouflage screen that was protecting a matt-black, diamond shaped craft. A craft that to anyone who had high enough security clearance to get close to, appeared like a black panther, ready to pounce off the dry lake bed and into the dark night.

Four levels beneath the lake bed, in the joint U.S. Military/NASA ultra-secret SMCC - Space Mission Control Center, NASA Flight Director; Commander Ross Channing, sat transfixed by the bank of monitors in front of him.

"Inertial measurement unit and pre-flight alignments confirmed," he said, speaking into the console.

T-5 minutes and counting…

The monitor in front of him, and digital clocks fixed to the white walls inside the control's clean room ticked down the launch sequence.

"Commencing transition to X40 on-board computers to launch configuration and starting fuel cell thermal conditioning," he said, wiping his brow. "Activating the flight recorders, crew members please close and lock visors."

He was one of only three people overseeing the top secret Moon mission – code-named Odyssey, from the secret, government underground launch base. The other two operatives remained silent, studying their launch computers, checking support systems and telemetry.

"Cross checking GAG's - Gravity Assist Gel suits. Systems functional and optimal," he confirmed.

Out on the lake bed, on-board the X40, were astronauts Colonel Bruce Bannister and Commander William Scott, who were seated across from each other in the command module of the sleek, black spacecraft, the most advanced ever built.

"Roger that," Bannister said, speaking into his space helmet mic, as he simultaneously checked the control panel on the arm of his GAG suit, a state-of-the-art advanced spacesuit that encapsulated the wearer with a special bio-gel to absorb the effects of inertia and gravity experienced during X40 flight.

"Sure is going to be one hell of a ride. Let's see what this thing can do," Scott replied, tapping the heat sensitive flight control screen on the control panel in front of him, as a pre-programmed flight plan flashed up in a brilliant blue onto the heads-up display.

"Plasma drive chamber looking good," Scott confirmed.

"Mag chamber online and good to go," Bannister said.

"Spy satellite free window is coming up in five seconds. Deuterium and tritium isotopes are fluid. She's all yours. God speed, and good luck to both of you. We'll see you back at Papoose at two a.m.," Channing said.

European, Russian, and Chinese satellite blackout is confirmed for the next four minutes. The X40 is cleared to go," the operative hunched over the computer bay confirmed.

T – 10 seconds...

"X40 transferring internal power from base to craft. Ground launch sequencer is go for auto sequence start. We are good to go," Bannister confirmed, checking the green lights strobing on the heads-up display.

"Activate main engine burn-off system. We have main plasma engine start," Channing confirmed.

Channing's monitor flashed. T – zero...

With the plasma drive engines glowing bright neon blue, the diamond-shaped craft accelerated along the vast dry lake bed before soaring off at a near vertical climb into the Nevada night sky, and reaching Earth's escape velocity of 35,505 feet per second, shortly after.

CHAPTER 20

ARMSTRONG, ALICIA, AND the two cameramen ran back up the forest track towards the campsite without looking back. They had no idea what had just happened, and didn't want to know. Before fleeing, Armstrong had spotted a spare M14 automatic weapon in the front of the Humvee, together with a radio, and had grabbed both.

The four of them reached the clearing after five minutes of running and collapsed onto the grass bank to catch their breath, close to where the fire was still smouldering.

"What the hell just happened, boss?" Alicia asked, as she drew in large gulps of air.

"I've no idea. I saw movement in the forest just before the flashes of light, but couldn't make anything out. It was too dark."

"You mean lasers. I saw them. They were bloody laser beams!" Doug shouted, his eyes wide with fear.

"That's what they looked like to me too," John agreed.

Armstrong shook his head. "None of this makes much sense, we need to get off this damn mountain, but we can't leave Bruce and the others up here, so this is what we're going to do –"

Before he could continue, John interrupted him. "Sod that. I'm not staying up here another second. I'm leaving now."

"I'm with you, John. We didn't sign up for this shit," Doug said, looking scared and pissed off.

"Listen guys, I'm feeling the same way, but we need to stick together, and we can't leave Bruce and the others up here can we?" Alicia pleaded.

"Please, everyone calm down. Alicia's right, we simply can't leave the others up here. We don't know what we're dealing with. We're going to have to go into that tunnel to find them. Then all drive back down to Shasta together," Armstrong ordered.

"I'm not hanging around here any longer. I'm going to take a leak then I'm leaving," John said.

"I'll join you."

John and Doug stood and walked over to where the Mercedes trucks were parked, close to the edge of the forest.

"Assholes," Alicia said, under her breath.

Although the sun had dropped below the horizon a good while ago, the peak of Mount Shasta, which loomed high above them, was still bathed in an orange glow, looking eerie but beautiful at the same time.

"The mineshaft might be the safest place to be," Alicia offered, tearing her eyes from the mountain and glancing towards the corrugated shack.

"I think you're –"

Armstrong was about to reply when a loud *crack* echoed across the clearing from the edge of the forest, close to where the boys were standing.

As Armstrong and Alicia looked over, a low, guttural Neanderthal growl echoed from the forest, as two ropes, fashioned into lassos, were flung out from the tree line and over the heads and shoulders of the two cameramen.

Still relieving themselves, the boys didn't have a chance to do anything as the ropes were pulled tight around their torsos and yanked taut, pulling them onto the ground, face down. Before Armstrong and Alicia could stand up, as if dragged by a powerful winch, the two guys disappeared, kicking and screaming in terror into the forest.

"Shit!" Armstrong screamed, grabbing the M14 and running towards the spot where the boys had been dragged in. He couldn't see a thing, but he unlocked the gun, and fired a few rounds into the treetops. The bullets tore into the pine trees, the noise of the gun drowning out the men's cries, and echoing up the mountain slopes and into the night sky.

Armstrong and Alicia stood at the edge of the forest, listening to the men's fading screams as they were dragged deeper into the dark forest.

Alicia grabbed Armstrong and started to shake and cry. "We're going to die up here."

"That's not going to happen," Armstrong said, still in shock. Surely the Bigfoot or whatever they were couldn't hunt humans like they were helpless animals? None of this made sense. Who the hell could have done that to the guys and why? Was it the U.S. Military, or the creatures? Not even the M14 he was gripping gave him comfort. They had to leave the clearing and quickly.

"Let's get the hell out of here. Run for the mine shaft, now!" Armstrong said.

Almost a mile farther along the dark tunnel, Tom, Jessica, and Bruce continued moving forward. The mysterious harpoon-like object was still giving off a slight glow, but it was slowly getting dimmer following the incident ten minutes earlier. They passed an old mining cart lying on its side, the wooden timbers it was constructed from still remarkably well preserved.

"It's definitely getting lighter," Jessica said, turning back to look at the old cart.

"I think you're right," Tom replied.

They continued for another minute or so in silence.

Suddenly, there was a faint buzzing, and Tom felt his mobile phone vibrate in his pocket. "What the hell? That's odd, I've got a signal," he said, stopping to yank the smartphone from his front pocket.

He checked the screen; it was a message from Gerry. The text was timed at 8.20 p.m., some ten minutes earlier.

GUYS, I HOPE YOU'RE ALL SAFE UP THERE ON THE MOUNTAIN. JUST TO LET YOU KNOW THE UN GENERAL ASSEMBLY ARE ABOUT TO MEET – 12 A.M. EASTERN TIME - TO DISCUSS THE SIGNAL, WHICH THE PRESS ARE NOW CONFIRMING IS ALIEN IN NATURE. THE SIGNAL APPARENTLY ORIGINATES FROM AN EARTH-LIKE PLANET IN THE CASSIOPEIA CONSTELLATION. THE PRESS ARE STATING THERE IS A COVER-UP OF MASSIVE PROPORTIONS GOING ON. AS YOU CAN IMAGINE, IT'S GOING NUTS IN WASHINGTON WITH PRESS AND CROWDS GROWING OUTSIDE THE WHITEHOUSE DEMANDING ANSWERS. THERE ARE SIMILAR SCENES OUTSIDE THE HOUSES OF PARLIAMENT OVER IN THE U.K.

GERRY.

"Jeez," Bruce whispered, after Tom had read out the message.

"I guess I might be able to get a Wi-Fi signal if your phone works," kneeling down and unzipped his laptop case and pulling out his computer, he hit the power button.

The laptop glowed white as it powered up. "Amazing, looks like I have an internet signal too, God knows how," he said, quickly searching for the United Nations homepage.

"Nothing surprises me about this place anymore," Tom muttered.

"Here we go, I think we can stream the UN meeting live," he said, turning the laptop around.

Tom and Jessica knelt down to get a better look, as the UN Emergency Meeting started to get underway at the United Nations in New York.

CHAPTER 21

UNITED NATIONS
SECURITY COUNCIL EMERGENCY MEETING
12 A.M. E.S.T.

THE U.N. SECURITY Council were gathering for their 8055th meeting in the Security Council's Chamber. The council's fifteen members had primary responsibility, under the UN Charter, for the maintenance of international peace and security, but only five were present for the midnight emergency meeting, called in response to the unfolding situation on Mount Shasta. The representatives present were from The United States, Russian Federation, Great Britain, China, and France.

The representatives were seated along one side of an oval, polished wood-panelled desk, fitted with state-of-the-art communications and computer terminals, which scrolled the translated speeches across each member's monitor as they spoke. Each country's national flag hung majestically on the panelled wall behind the respective representative.

U.S. Ambassador Nicky Harker nodded to President Trent, who was seated next to her and observing the meeting, stood up, and started to address the assembly. "I have to admit I never considered that I would be addressing the assembly on this subject, but I must say it makes a nice break from discussing Syria, or indeed North Korea," she said, dryly.

The other four permanent members nodded their heads, agreeing to her sentiment.

"As you all know, a post-detection protocol, a set of structured rules, standards, guidelines if you like, which government entities should ideally follow in the event of the detection of confirmed signals from extra-terrestrial civilizations has been drawn up. Though not formally adopted by any government, the U.S. position is that we should stick with the *Declaration of Principles Concerning Activities Following the Detection of Extra-terrestrial Intelligence*." Ambassador Harker paused to take a sip of water, her mouth suddenly becoming unpleasantly dry.

She put her glass down and continued her address. "The protocol was developed by the International Academy of Astronautics, with the support of the International Institute of Space Law, in conjunction with research from SETI, who as you all know detected the signal. METI, Messaging to Extra-terrestrial Intelligence, and CETI, Communication with Extra-terrestrial Intelligence were also involved." Harker paused to make sure the members were still following what she was saying. They all were.

She carried on. "Scientists studying this field have argued that the formulation of post-detection protocols can be guided by three main factors: Society's readiness to accept the news that an alien signal has been detected; how the news of detection is released, and the comprehensibility of the message in the signal."

Russian Ambassador Victor Charski interrupted Ambassador Harker. "This is all very well, but as I understand it, we have no idea what this signal says yet, or indeed if it's even genuine!"

Harker nodded. "That is correct, but these protocols are the best framework we have at the moment and the U.S. position is that they be implemented and followed to the letter."

"We will see about that," Charski responded, sitting back down.

Harker nodded at the Russian ambassador, before continuing her lengthy address. "The council needs to consider the range of likely reactions from the press, various religious groups, political leaders, and the general public. The differences in reactions across the range of cultural and religious boundaries, as you might imagine, will be substantial. Press agencies all around the world are already getting hold of the story, and people are naturally starting to panic and they need answers to many and varied questions."

Chinese Ambassador Zing stood and addressed the council. "The Chinese position is that this contact, if indeed it is genuine, should be framed as a positive development that will benefit all humankind. Removal of extremist group websites and other forms of social media needs immediate address. Our fear is that such terrorist groups could start attacking this discovery as being evil or immoral. It is possible that this would spark attempts to terminate communication by interfering with the signal or targeting the detecting technology with cyber-attacks." Ambassador Zing sat back down.

"Thank you for that useful input," Ambassador Harker said, smiling at Zing, before continuing her speech. "There is much we need to consider here today. The nature of a response, if any, once we have been able to decode the signal, needs consideration. We are aware that SETI is concerned with how humankind should carry out this communication, and whether a response should be with one collective voice, or if anyone with access to a transmitter should have the right to communicate."

"Clearly that would be inappropriate," the Russian ambassador said.

Harker nodded, acknowledging the objection. "Any response would need to be carefully crafted by the council, on behalf of all humankind. Several options exist, including a description of our species and planet, much like the discs that were sent out on the Voyager probes, a request for information for example. All this must be considered very quickly," Harkin said, retaking her seat in front of President Trent.

Ambassador James Horsey stood up. "May I say thank you to our American friends for such a concise briefing on this rather unusual situation we find ourselves in. From the British standpoint, when considering post-detection courses of action, we need to consider the relative technological capabilities both in relation to signal relay time and whether or not the senders of the signal are thought to pose a militaristic threat. If the transmission is coming from outside the solar system, which I understand it is, there will be a significant lag in time between transmission and receipt by either party, unless of course, some exotic or unknown technology is being used to transmit and receive the signals. The potential disparities in sophistication of weapons technology hold grave implications for how humankind should react. I believe the council will be aware of British theoretical physicist, Stephen Hawking's view, which is that we can't risk revealing the precise location of the Earth to alien civilizations who might want to destroy us."

Ambassador Harker rose to her feet again. "Yes, thank you, Ambassador Horsey. As the council appreciate, the United States take such a threat incredibly seriously, hence the reason why we already have a military presence on the ground on Mount Shasta, where the signal was first detected. Council members, it would appear that whoever is sending the signal, already knows we are here."

A hushed silence fell over the chamber at that point, the permanent members remained seated, transfixed to their computer monitors, which now revealed the latest information on the signal, live pictures of the Cobalt Ridge Glacier, together with info-graphics showing Mount Shasta and the region of the Moon where the signal appeared to terminate, and a representation of the second signal from the same location on the Moon, to star HR 8832 in the constellation of Cassiopeia.

Ambassador Harker stood to address the assembly again. "The United States is happy to adopt the following principles drawn up by SETI," she said, as a petite dark-haired female handed each of the members a manila envelope containing a number of documents.

"The papers before you all have been endorsed by six international, professional space societies and they constitute an informal agreement proposing a set of nine post-detection protocols. I can summarise the important protocols as follows," Harker said, reaching for her water again to lubricate her dry throat.

She continued reading. "Consultations on whether a message should be sent, and its content, should take place within the Committee on the Peaceful Uses of Outer Space of the United Nations. These consultations should be open to participation by all interested States and should be intended to lead to recommendations reflecting a consensus." Ambassador Harker paused to allow the members to turn to the correct page in the document.

She continued. "The United Nations General Assembly should consider making the decision on whether or not to send a message to the extra-terrestrial intelligence in the first place, and on what the content of that message should be, based on recommendations from the Committee on the Peaceful Uses of Outer Space and from governmental and non-governmental organisations. If a decision is made to send a message, it should be sent on behalf of all humankind, rather than from individual States," she said, eying each of the members over the rim of her glasses.

"The content of such a message should reflect a careful concern for the broad interests and wellbeing of humanity, and should be made available to the public in advance of transmission. No communication to extra-terrestrial intelligence should be sent by any State until appropriate international consultations have taken place. States should not cooperate with attempts to communicate with extra-terrestrial intelligence that do not conform to the principles of this declaration. And finally, States participating in this declaration and United Nations bodies should draw on the expertise of scientists, scholars, and other persons with relevant knowledge."

The Russian ambassador stood again. "Thank you, Ambassador Harker for that detailed account of the position with regards to...to the unusual situation that is unfolding in northern California. May I just say that I think it important and prudent that we also put together a joint military unit, with representatives from all the five permanent members, to be deployed at ground zero in case something unexpected occurs. Heaven knows we have seen enough American science fiction movies to make us all a little concerned about what is happening," he said, raising his eyebrows at the delegation before him, before retaking his seat.

Ambassador Harker went to stand again, but President Trent placed his hand on her shoulders and stood himself.

"Ambassador Charski, delegate members, I speak on behalf of the American nation here and on the very unnatural events currently taking place on American soil over in California. I can't speak for our Hollywood friends, who have been in the entertainment business for the last century, but I can tell you that I am taking this very seriously. At the present time, I believe that our armed forces can handle any issue that arises over on the mountain, but I thank you for your suggestion Ambassador," Trent said, retaking his seat.

CHAPTER 22

THE THREE OF them watched the streaming video of the UN Security Council meeting in silence, just a distant *drip...drip...drip...*echoed along the mineshaft as the video flickered and went blank.

"Well that's just great. They're talking as if this thing is a genuine signal from aliens from outer space and we're walking along a bloody tunnel right under the mountain from where the signal has been detected!" Jessica complained.

Tom would be lying if he said he wasn't also feeling a little afraid, but this could be the discovery of the century. He tried to think rationally about the events, but it wasn't easy. *Were the Bigfoot sightings/activity related to the mystery signal, or was it just coincidence?* It was hard to believe that the two supernatural events weren't somehow related, but how on earth could they be? "Well, it's incredible for sure. Just think what it could mean for the human race if the signal were genuine. We'd have the chance to learn about the evolution of another species from another planet. We could be enriched with technological knowledge beyond our wildest dreams, maybe learn how to exist as a species without blowing ourselves up. Learn about other sentient beings in our galaxy, maybe even outside it. I mean it's what dreams are made of," Tom proclaimed, as the three of them set off again along the lightening tunnel.

Jess rolled her eyes. "I can't believe you think about all that rubbish," she said.

Bruce cleared his throat. "I don't know dude, but it would make a great science fiction movie."

Tom checked the harpoon device in his backpack. The ultra-violet glow had all but faded. "It seems safe at least. Come on, let's try find the cavern, check it out and get the hell out of here."

Jess smiled. "Now I like the sound of that!"

Three-quarters of a mile behind, Armstrong and Alicia moved quickly along the mineshaft. "Boss," Alicia said, her voice hoarse with fear, and her eyes bloodshot from lack of sleep and tears. "Do you think those things followed us in here?"

Armstrong tried not to think of the possibility. He was still shocked over the way John and Doug had been yanked off their feet and pulled ferociously into the forest. And the trap set for the vehicles. Had it been prepared for them for when they returned back down the mountain? A shiver raced up his spine at the thought.

"I bloody hope not. But don't worry we have this," he said, holding up the M14 he'd taken from the front of the Humvee.

"Well just make sure something doesn't sneak up behind us, like it did with poor John and Doug," Alicia said, her voice shaky with emotion.

Armstrong had to admit that he'd never felt quite so scared in his life, as they hurried along the dark mine shaft. He continuously checked the passage behind him using the M14's night vision scope, which turned the blackness into an eerie green colour. So far, they remained alone.

The wind was starting to pick up and blow clouds of frozen snow particles down the eastern face of Mount Shasta towards the Cobalt Ridge Glacier. The military team had just finished setting up a prefab hut, complete with computer and satellite transmitter for the task ahead. U.S army personnel from the second Humvee had moved crates of equipment from the vehicle and were now opening them under a weatherproof tarp they'd erected.

Dr Lucy Davies and Professor Beck looked on from their position close to the glacial area where the signal was being transmitted, the hoods on their parkas pulled tight around their faces against the biting wind.

Tom, Jess, and Bruce continued along the mineshaft, which was now almost light enough for them to walk along without a flashlight. "I can see something up ahead," Tom said, pointing to a feature that appeared out of place in relation to the architecture of the tunnel they'd been walking along for the last mile or so.

"What is it?" Jessica whispered.

Tom turned his flashlight back on and directed it at the feature. The light from the torch washed over it and revealed the intersecting mineshaft shown on the internet map and on the old parchment.

"I thought it looked odd, it's the other tunnel that leads directly towards the cavern. According to the map it's about another two-hundred feet farther along," Tom explained.

"It's weird. I just don't understand how it's getting lighter," Jessica added.

"The only explanation I have is that there is a natural light source coming from somewhere," but even Tom wasn't convinced about his idea.

The three of them proceeded cautiously towards the intersection and when they reached it, Tom directed the flashlight away from the mountain and down the long, dark tunnel that intersected the tunnel they were in. It looked the same. To the right, however, the solid, rock walls appeared to be glistening from the mystery light source emanating from farther along the shaft.

"Very unusual; It might be coming from the quartz crystals in the rock," Tom suggested.

"It's beautiful," Jess whispered, somewhat in awe.

"Did you know that the Ancient Greeks referred to quartz as *krustallos*, derived from the Ancient Greek word, *kruos* which means *icy cold*. Some philosophers apparently believed the mineral to be a form of super-cooled ice," Bruce said, matter-of-factly.

"Nice little fact and kind of appropriate seeing as there's tons of the stuff above our heads," Tom said.

"Now, how would you know something as useless as that?" Jess asked, shaking her head.

"Read it online when I was searching about the mineshafts today," Bruce smirked.

"Are we good to go?" Tom asked, feeling impatient.

Bruce nodded. "Let's do it."

"We've come this far. Let's go and find out where the hell the light is coming from," Jessica agreed.

"I'm glad your sense of adventure has returned." Tom checked the time. Thirty minutes had passed since the UN meeting in New York. "Come on, let's go."

CHAPTER 23

THE MOON

September 20, 2 A.M., PT

ASTRONAUTS COLONEL BRUCE Bannister and Commander William Scott carried out a series of pre-landing systems checks as the X40 approached the Moon at a velocity of 75,000 mph, almost three times the speed of the Apollo space craft almost fifty years earlier. The screen on the console in front of them confirmed they'd covered 215,000 miles, leaving just under 25,000 miles before reaching lunar orbit.

"This is Groom Lake calling Odyssey. We hope you guys had a good trip up there. We are showing fifteen seconds to plasma engine brake and lunar orbit insertion," Mission Flight Commander Ross Channing's calm voice, sounded from the control panel.

"Roger that. We have a spectacular view of our blue planet and all you guys back home. Acknowledge lunar orbit insertion. We are good for plasma engine brake," Scott said.

"Prepare for plasma drive deceleration in five...four...three...two...one," Bannister confirmed.

"Coming up on the ten-thousand mile mark to target. Checking lunar entry and orbit configuration," Scott replied.

The X40's plasma engine reverse thrusters fired, slowing the craft down from its cruising speed to a lunar orbit entry velocity of 15,000 mph.

There was a brief pause before Channing's voice sounded over the coms. "Roger that Odyssey. All systems are looking good from down here."

"Lunar orbit in thirty seconds," Scott said, tapping the computer in front of him, and double checking the landing coordinates.

"Lunar orbit insertion confirmed," Bannister said.

The X40's plasma drive engines glowed blue as they kicked in once again to control the craft down as it approached the Moon.

"All systems nominal, we are good to go for lunar orbit insertion."

"Roger that," Channing confirmed.

The X40's conventional rocket thrusters fired, making the necessary adjustments, sending the craft on the correct descent trajectory for lunar orbit insertion.

"Pitch and roll adjustment confirmed. We are entering lunar orbit in five...four...three...two...one." As he said it, Scott peered out of craft's small triangular window. "What a sight! Passing over the Sea of Tranquillity in...ten seconds."

"Roger that," Channing confirmed, over the coms from Groom Lake base. "Do you have visual on the Moon's surface? Can you see anything unusual up there?"

"Negative," Scott replied, after a few seconds.

The X40's video rolled as the craft passed over 00.67408° north latitude, 23.47297° east longitude at twelve thousand mph., the *Mare Tranquillitatis* region, better known as the *Sea of Tranquillity*, the landing site for the 1969 Apollo mission.

"Confirmed, all looks good down at *Statio Tranquillitatis*," Scott said, referring to the Latin name given to the Apollo landing site, after Neil Armstrong's now legendary commentary shortly after Apollo landed - *Houston, Tranquillity Base here. The Eagle has landed.*

"Okay plasma engine brake on my mark in, five...four...three...two...one," Scott said, his eyes darting from the computer screen to the side window, and the view of Earth a quarter of a million miles away. The X40's thrusters slowed the craft further to the appropriate Moon orbit velocity of 35,505 feet per second.

"Groom Lake to Odyssey, we are picking up some minor coms disturbance. Do your systems showing any interference at all?" Flight Director Channing asked.

"Ah that's a negative, Groom. Nothing showing here," Scott said, checking the blue array in front of them.

"We'll keep an eye on that. Please commence auto landing sequence," came the response.

"Aha, Roger that. Adjustments for auto landing sequence confirmed," Scott said, tapping the console.

The astronauts monitored the screen as the X40 rolled to the right as it altered its orbit slightly to take them over the far side of the Moon and their final descent near the *Saha Impact Crater.*

"Roll executed, entering far side orbit now," Scott confirmed.

"Roger that. Estimated ten minutes to landing," Channing replied.

"Ten minutes, check," Scott said, as the X40 slowed down to 2500 mph as it went into orbit over the dark, far side of the Moon.

"Picking up more coms interference," Scott confirmed.

"Roger that. It's expected," Channing replied, his voice barely discernible through the crackling static.

"Telemetry is looking good. Pitch and roll landing auto sequence start in five...four...three...two...one," Bannister said, nodding at Scott.

"Well here goes. Let's hope there's no landing party waiting for us," Bannister joked.

"I wouldn't bank on it," Scott replied, his voice tense, as the X40 slowed further and commenced a forty-five degree roll to prepare for the auto landing sequence.

"Plasma engine shut down. Descent sequence in five...four...three...two...one," Scott confirmed.

The X40 executed a further roll and rotated so that its underbelly was falling under controlled descent to the Moon's surface, and heading towards the landing site, a relatively flat basalt plain half a mile from the *Saha Impact Crater.*

The view from the flight deck was serene. The Earth was reflecting the light from the sun, which was presently behind it, giving the Earth the appearance of a distant crescent in the blackness of space.

"Ten seconds to touchdown," Scott confirmed his voice tense with nerves as telemetry scrolled down the screens in front of them. The X40's thrusters continued to make minute adjustments as the descent computer brought the craft down.

The screen counted down the height to the surface in feet; 80...60...40...20...5.

"All engines shut off," Bannister confirmed.

The final few seconds ticked by as if they were minutes, until suddenly the X40's landing computer screen lit up red. Touchdown!

Scott and Bannister looked at each other and both sighed in relief.

"This is spacecraft Odyssey, safely down on the *Saha plateau,*" Scott spoke into the coms, hoping Groom Base was picking up the transmission, relief evident in his voice.

Silence.

"Wow! That was one hell of a ride," Bannister said, wiping his brow.

"Okay, let's do a full systems check and get the mission underway."

Scott nodded, as he reached out for the touch screen console to run through the post-landing sequence checks.

Twenty minutes later, both astronauts were standing on the exit ramp next to the two-man lunar rover, which contained an assortment of sensitive measuring equipment that had been provided to them for the mission to analyse the mystery signal, chemical analysis of ejecta near the crater, and such like.

"Pressurising exit compartment now," Scott said, pressing a glowing green button.

With the airlock engaged, the exit hatch slowly opened. Back at Groom Lake, a loud clunk had resonated into the compartment when this procedure had been practised, but in space, there was just silence. All Scott could hear was the steady *thumping* of his own heartbeat.

The hatch slowly opened, and the ramp automatically deployed, allowing both astronauts to walk out onto the Moon's surface. Bannister operated the rover remotely, using the control pad fitted into the wrist section of his suit.

Small puffs of grey dust fanned out from their footfall as they stepped off the ramp and onto the Moon's surface.

The sight that greeted them both was truly awe inspiring. The far side of the Moon, shielded from any light from the Sun or Earth, meant that the field of stars visible to them in the Milky Way Galaxy was mesmerising.

"It's just awash with stars. It's incredible. It's all just a sheet of white," Scott said, gazing out into space. As he stared at the field of white, his heart started to beat faster, reminding him of their mission. Each pin-prick of light, literally billions of them, was a sun. Each sun, almost without doubt, was orbited by its own planets, and each extra-solar planetary system, potentially had its own habitable planets. It seemed impossible to him that humankind was all alone in the galaxy, let alone the universe, as he dragged his gaze away from the stars.

CHAPTER 24

Mount Shasta, 2 A.M.

"WHAT'S THAT SOUND?" Lucy shouted above the biting wind whistling down the eastern slope of Mount Shasta where she and Professor Beck were shielding themselves behind the large, rocky outcrop that encircled the Cobalt Ridge Glacier.

Beck cocked his head and listened for a few seconds. "I can't hear anything apart from the wind."

Standing guard, the military team were still spread out in a large semi-circle around the top of the glacial area, large spot lights that had been set up around the location lit up the entire area, two of them appearing to speak into their headsets.

Above the wind, the low, continuous rumble echoed down the slopes of the mountain again and into the valley below. This time it was unmistakable. The low continuous rumble echoed down the slopes and into the valley below.

"Jesus, what was that?" Lucy asked, a look of anxiety spreading over her face.

Beck shook his head. "I'm not sure, but I have a bad feeling about this. Mount Shasta is a dormant volcano, right? Perhaps she's waking up?"

"Please don't say that, not when we're about to make the greatest discovery of our time."

Lieutenant Coffey Jordan, who was talking to one of the soldiers, looked over at them from the tree line, and started speaking into his radio for a minute or so, before heading over to the outcrop of rock where Lucy and Beck were standing.

"Okay you two, I've have been authorised to tell you that the Odyssey mission is underway on the Moon. The two-man team is en route to the *Saha Impact Crater* as we speak and we have been placed on standby to commence Cobalt Ridge Glacier insertion. We will be melting our way into the glacier to insert fibre optics, which I believe was your idea Dr Davies?"

"Ah, yes," Lucy said, a mixture of excitement and fear in her voice. As she spoke, another rumble echoed along the ridge, this time, not from the mountain, but from a third military vehicle that had just pulled up.

"That's the additional equipment arriving," Jordan said, as his headset crackled to life.

Lucy and Professor Beck looked on as another team of military men, dressed in white and green camouflage uniforms, started unloading large crates of equipment from the third vehicle, before carrying it past them along the ridge to the glacier, dropping them just beyond the outcrop of rocks.

Lucy watched as the men broke open the crates, began assembling what looked like a giant barrel-shaped gun mounted on a tripod, and pulled thick cables from another crate and connected them to the device. Two men then carried the other end of the cables back to the vehicle, presumably to connect up to a power supply. Lucy guessed the device was some kind of laser.

Another rumble rolled down the ridge, this time from the mountain again, causing the six-man military team to stop work and take cover as loose rocks and snow rained down from above, the device they'd been setting up suddenly lurching to one side as it was hit by a melon-sized boulder.

Lucy and Professor Beck ducked behind the largest of the granite rocks that formed a ring around the location of the signal, to protect themselves from the falling debris.

"Jeez it's getting a bit dangerous out here. Any more of this and I think we'll have to call it a day," Beck shouted.

"No chance. I know it's nearly three in the morning but we can't let the military take control out here, you know that," Lucy replied.

With the imminent danger seemingly now gone, the pair of them got up from their crouched positions and moved closer to where the device was being realigned by the military. Two of the men had now tethered the laser with a thin metal cord. One end of which was being secured to one of the nearest pine trees and the other to a flat plateaux of rock, using a piton. The laser device was now being pulled taut by the men, and safe from being knocked over by any falling debris.

Lieutenant Jordan walked back over to them. "Okay, we're on standby from Washington to commence the operation. In case you're wondering about the device, it's the latest Lockheed Martin 10 kW mobile laser. It will take just a few seconds to burn a four- centimetre diameter column through the glacier and bedrock underneath and into the cavern. The depth has been set to the exact thickness of ice and rock, so there's no possibility of causing any damage to whatever is down there."

Before Lucy could respond, his sat-phone came to life with a burst of static. He yanked it from his belt clip and raised it to his ear. "Okay, Roger that. Good to go. Thank you general, we'll power her up and have some live video for you in five minutes," he said, shouting into the sat-phone, as he turned around, raised his arm, and made a rapid circular motion with his fist to the military team standing around the laser device.

"We have orders to go in," he said. "You guys, just please stand back and watch the show."

CHAPTER 25

TOM, JESSICA, AND Bruce had been waiting nervously for what seemed like half an hour before emerging from the small alcove in the tunnel where they'd been sheltering. Tom feared there had been a collapse somewhere in the mineshaft, but after the third rumble he realised the sound was more likely to be volcanic in nature, not that it made things any better.

"Come on, let's move on quickly," Tom said, as they walked with renewed vigour along the ever lightening intersecting shaft towards the cavern shown on the old map.

Suddenly, there was a loud *crack*. "Damn it," Jessica cursed, as she took her foot off something she'd just stepped on.

"What have you done?" Tom asked, feeling his nerves fray.

"I don't know," Jess said, looking down to inspect the ground. "What the hell is it?" she whispered.

Tom turned his flashlight on and shone it down to Jess' feet. As the light washed over the earth where Jessica had stepped, an off-white strip became visible. The object had snapped in two. Tom knelt down and immediately realised what it was; a rib bone.

"Ugh, what the hell is that doing in here?" Jessica asked, stepping back.

Tom panned the beam of light along the floor of the mineshaft, seeing there wasn't just one rib bone, but tens, maybe hundreds of them, scattered along the tunnel as far as they could see, mainly on the ground along both sides of the mineshaft.

"What the hell?" Bruce said, his jaw dropping open.

"Why are there so many bones in here?" Jess whispered, raising her hands to her mouth in shock.

"I'm not quite sure. It doesn't make sense. It's illogical that so many animals would wander down here and just die," Tom said.

"Well, come on, guys, do you expect anything to make any freaking sense?" Bruce added.

Tom could see ribs, femurs, entire rib cages partly crushed, and farther along the passage, skulls of various mountain animals, including deer, stag, and foxes. "Jesus, there's something quite large farther up," Tom said, directing the flashlight on the silhouette of some dead animal thirty feet farther along the tunnel.

"Can't we just go back?" Jess pleaded. I couldn't give a damn any longer about what's in the cavern. I just want to get the hell out of here."

"Quiet! What's that noise?" Bruce suddenly said, raising his forefinger to his lips, turning around and looking down the dark tunnel they'd just walked along.

Tom's heart started to pound in his chest. Were they about to suffer the same fate as the creatures whose bones littered the ground? Tom panned the tunnel with his flashlight. He could sense something. Bruce was right, something was moving along the tunnel towards them.

The flashlight's beam washed over a broken section of wall in the mineshaft, on the left side, twenty feet farther along. "Quick, head for that crack," Tom whispered, as they made a dash for the damaged section of wall.

The three of them squeezed into the space, and Tom snapped the flashlight off. The natural light, quartz, and iron pyrite embedded in the passage walls left the tunnel illuminated, as if in an ethereal, gloomy twilight.

The sound of heavy footfall and grunting became louder.

"Those creatures followed us in here, I know they did. We're screwed," Jessica sobbed, her body trembling.

Tom knew Jess was right. They were trapped.

Suddenly, there was a loud, *crack* as something stepped on one of the bones, twenty feet along the tunnel, just as Jess had done.

"What the hell is this?" A familiar voice echoed along the passage towards them.

Was that Armstrong? Tom turned the flashlight on, squeezed out of the hiding place, and shone the beam of light in the direction of the sound. Standing next to each other, bent over double as they tried to catch their breath, were Alicia and Armstrong.

"Bloody hell! Thank God, it's you guys. Are you alright? What the hell happened back there?" Tom queried, feeling massive relief at seeing the two of them standing there.

Bruce and Jess stepped out from the recess. Bruce ran over to the pair of them and gave Alicia and his boss a hug.

"Steady on, Bruce, I wasn't gone that long," Armstrong said, managing to make light of their predicament. "Seriously, we are damn glad to find you three. You'll never believe what happened to us back in the forest. On top of that, we're convinced one or more of the creatures might have followed us in here. That's why we've been running, despite having this," he said, referring to the M14 he was still gripping.

"Seriously, it's not funny. There's no way I'll be doing anymore TV stuff, unless it's for the QVC channel," Alicia said, trying to catch her breath.

"What the hell are all these bones doing here?" Armstrong finally asked, looking along the tunnel, still trying to catch his breath.

"We don't know. It's very odd. There's something larger on the ground a little farther up too. We should all move. The cavern can't be that far away. There might even be a way out as there seems to be natural light coming from somewhere," he added.

"I agree. Let's just keep going," Armstrong panted.

There was no sign or sound coming from the passage behind them. If the creatures were following, they didn't appear to be close.

The five of them moved forward, passing the damaged section of wall. Tom then focussed the flashlight on the dark silhouette farther up on the right. As they approached it, Tom felt a column of ice race up his spine as he realised what the large dark mass was.

"Shit. I don't want to alarm you guys more than you already are but I think this is our bear friend from the forest," he said, directing the flashlight onto the dead animal, and its missing forearm.

Jessica put her hands up to her mouth. "Jeez it stinks," she mumbled.

"Well that's just great. It means those creatures are using this mine shaft for their den and we're walking right up to their dinner table!" she said.

Tom tried to make sense of what was going on. Bigfoot, if that's what they were, in the system of tunnels that led to the location from where a signal was apparently being transmitted to the Moon. *What the hell was going on?* "Is the weapon loaded?" he asked Armstrong.

"Damn right," he replied, without taking his eyes off the dead bear.

The five of them moved quickly past the dead animal, Bruce filming the scene as they went.

The tunnel continued to get noticeably lighter from a strange, light blue glow that was originating from somewhere nearby. The scattered bones on the ground grew noticeably less as they moved forward, having just been concentrated near the damaged section of the mine.

The mineshaft ahead now curved around to the right, the dimensions of the tunnel getting larger the closer they got to the light source.

"This is just so eerie, man," Bruce said, panning the movie camera around the glistening walls of the tunnel. "What the hell is going on with your hair?" he suddenly said, pointing at Tom's head and filming what he was witnessing.

Everyone stopped and looked at Tom, who was about five paces ahead of them all. His hair had started to stand on end, as if it were full of static. Tom raised his hand to his hair, suddenly sensing the static charge, then noticed the same was happening to Jess' and Alicia's hair, it was as if they were in a wind tunnel.

"Static electricity, there's an energy source of some kind. It must be coming from the cavern. I can hear a faint buzzing now too," Tom said.

"Hold on a moment," Armstrong said, as he stopped and pulled the magazine out of the M14. "We haven't got much ammo left, so I'm setting the gun to a three round burst mode."

"Good idea, this sure would be a bad time to run low on bullets," Bruce replied.

"Come on, let's keep going. It can't be much farther now," Tom said, grabbing Jess' hand.

They walked around the curved section of tunnel, the electrical buzz getting louder, reminding Tom of the noise a large electricity pylon gave off on a wet day back in the U.K.

Suddenly, there was a pulse of bright blue light, followed by a loud pop of electrical discharge. "Get down!" Tom shouted, as they all threw themselves to the ground, fearing an explosion.

"Ouch, my bloody wrist," Alicia cried.

"What the hell was that?" Bruce asked.

"Is everybody okay? There's an electrical power source just up ahead. It's giving off plenty of static but as long as there's no water around we should be okay."

"Oh that's great! Don't forget there's a tonne of frozen water above our heads," Jess said.

Tom got to his feet. "Hopefully it will stay in that form. Come on, it's time to find out what's really going on."

Up ahead was a kink in the passage, caused by a huge slab of granite that the builders of the mine a hundred years ago must have found too hard to move. The blue glow was coming from the other side of it.

"Let me go in first, Tom," Armstrong said, gripping the M14.

"Good idea. We don't appear to have been followed," Tom said, directing his flashlight into the dark, but thankfully empty tunnel, behind.

Armstrong moved forward, through the narrow gap and into what they assumed must be the cavern beyond, with the girls followed quickly behind, and then Tom with Bruce last.

Tom squeezed past the giant slab of granite and into the space beyond where the other four were staring at something, their mouths half open, eyes wide in what Tom could only describe as a look of wonder mixed with fear.

They were standing in a large, circular, dome-shaped cavern, approximately thirty feet across, and a similar size in depth. The cavern roof rose to about fifteen feet above them and was two thirds solid granite and around a third solid ice, turquoise in colour, part of the Cobalt Ridge Glacier above.

Lying on the ground, where the sides of the cavern rose from the solid granite floor, were several recognisable items. A number of old picks, lanterns, hammers, piles of old rope, and lying on its side, an old, wooden mining cart; just some of the tools and items of equipment used by the miners that once worked in the tunnels.

It wasn't this that Tom and his friends were staring at in bewilderment however. Half entombed in the turquoise ice, as if being slowly revealed as the glacier above melted, was some kind of device, or machine. It was hard to describe, but Tom doubted he was looking at anything that had originated on Earth. The device was black, but appeared to change from gloss to matte and then weirdly to a translucent black, which appeared to show the turquoise glacier behind it.

The device was humming and giving off an indigo/blue glow, then bright, white, light and was pulsating slightly. On the cavern floor, beneath the object, was a pile of sleek, shiny metallic-coloured objects. It took Tom a few seconds to register what they were. They were the harpoon-like devices that they'd found in the forest, at least a hundred of them, lying in a pile under the device.

"My God!" Tom said, removing his backpack to check the device was still in his pack. It was, and not only that, it was starting to glow again.

Before any of them could speak, a blue haze started to appear around the device, filling the cavern, top to bottom directly ahead of them. The hum coming from the object started increasing in intensity and then, as if they were watching some weird special effect in a science fiction movie, a tennis ball-sized, ovoid, jet-black hole opened up in the blue light field, becoming larger by the second, until it was about ten feet in length and five feet in height. Then there was a flash of silver and one of the harpoon-like objects appeared from the black space and dropped out, landing on the pile that had formed on the ground. As the ovoid started to diminish in size, something else appeared to emerge from the black space, this time, a dark, solid, shape.

The dark mass appeared to be moving, and was levitating in an aura of blue haze inside the black eye. As it emerged from the black void, Tom could see that the thing was alive.

It landed on the ground to the right of the mound of harpoon-like devices with a *thud*. The black oval then winked out, leaving a haze of blue in its place once more.

"What in the world...?" Bruce uttered, as the two girls screamed at the sight in front of them.

Lying on the floor, clearly confused, and possibly injured, was what appeared to be one of the Bigfoot creatures. It tried to stand, but staggered and fell as its legs buckled beneath it. It then saw the five of them looking at it from the opposite end of the cavern, and let out a painful sounding growl, quickly scrambled back onto its feet—this time maintaining its balance—and stumbled towards them.

"Shoot the fucking thing!" Tom shouted, turning to Armstrong, feeling as if time had inexplicably slowed down.

Armstrong raised the M14, and squeezed the trigger, but nothing happened.

"It's jammed!" he screamed, as the creature lurched forward.

CHAPTER 26

THE MOON

Far side, *Saha Impact Crater*

THE TWO ASTONAUTS guided the lunar rover around the crater wall of an ancient meteor impact crater, and across a debris-free section of anorthosite rock—a calcium-rich type of rock found in abundance on the Moon.

The backdrop of brilliant, white stars hadn't ceased to amaze the men as they both continued to stare in awe at the magnificent sight.

A high resolution video camera mounted on the rover was recording the entire mission. A similar camera, one of the many array of instruments mounted on the X40 had filmed the astronauts as they left the vicinity of the landing site and headed out towards the *Saha Impact Crater*.

"Can you hear that?" Bannister asked, referring to a deep, continuous hum that had become increasingly evident inside his space helmet. The sound, he knew wasn't anything that they were hearing from the Moon, as of course they were in a vacuum, but it must be some interference they were picking up from within their own communications systems.

"Affirmative, some kind of background interference up here," Scott replied.

Bannister guided the rover down a steep, thirty-foot bank, its wheels kicking up grey dust as the vehicle's large wheels spun momentarily, as they lost grip on the Moon's surface. A glowing red dot was now visible on the rover's navigation screen, the vehicle's auto-guidance system now taking the astronauts to the location of the mystery signal and the eastern edge of the ancient impact crater.

The steep bank gave way to another wide, flat section of breccia rock. The matrix of different materials, minerals, and fragments clearly evident in the breccia as the rover travelled over it.

"Interference becoming more intense," Scott said, as the rover manoeuvred between two twenty-foot diameter impact craters.

The navigation screen on the rover confirmed that they were now only three-hundred feet from the edge of the crater.

They travelled across the *Saha Plateau* for another two hundred feet or so before the rover made a right turn and headed towards a steep bank that formed the outer rim of the crater.

"Sixty feet to crater rim," Bannister confirmed.

"Picking up increasing levels of static," Scott replied.

The rover proceeded across an area strewn with small boulders, ejecta from the meteor impact that took place millions, perhaps billions of years ago.

Suddenly, a brilliant flash of blue light erupted from the crater ahead before vanishing again.

"Jesus, did you just see that?" Scott gasped, breathing heavily. The monitor on the arm of his space suit showing his vital signs confirmed his heart rate had just jumped to 190 bpm.

"Affirmative. It would appear that we're not alone up here," Bannister replied, the tone of his voice tense.

The rover reached the bank of the crater and proceeded up the outer rim until a boulder field made any closer approach impossible.

"Looks like we need to make the final approach on foot," Scott panted.

The rover's monitor confirmed the signal source was just twenty-five feet ahead, inside the ancient impact crater.

As the rover came to a halt, Scott powered it down, and set it to solar recharge, ensuring the movie camera remained on.

From the compartment at the rear of the rover, the astronauts grabbed the equipment given to them during the mission briefing back at the Groom Lake base, before looking up at the crater rim and the eerie, blue glow that was now coming from somewhere inside the ancient impact site.

"Are you ready?" Scott asked Bannister over the static.

Bannister wasn't ready. He'd been concerned as soon as he'd left the briefing room back at Groom Lake. The fact that they'd been made aware that NASA had been monitoring certain 'activity' on the surface of the Moon that needed urgent investigation had started alarm bells ringing. He couldn't show his fear otherwise he'd have been removed from the mission and never gotten this ride to the moon, something that he and every astronaut longed for.

Bannister simply nodded, his anxiety plain to see as a trickle of sweat ran down his forehead.

The two astronauts left the rover and started clambering up the eastern ridge to the crater rim.

The canvas of bright, white stars spanning the horizon beyond the crater rim and above them was now intermittently coloured blue, from the weird glow emanating from the crater.

Bannister felt his heart racing as he realised that what they were about to discover had to be alien in origin.

The *Saha Crater* was around sixty-six miles in circumference, its rim on the plateaux side elevated thirty-feet above the Moon's surface; regolith ejected from the impact zone and formed at the time of the meteor strike. The slope leading to the rim was strewn with tektites, obelisk-shaped rock, melted into glass from the energy created by the impactor meteorite.

The astronauts reached the crater rim together, the blue glow enveloping the glass visors of their space helmets as they peered into the crater.

What they saw captivated them. Within the crater, and close to the eastern side, was what appeared to be a device of some sort, about the size of a truck, dark in colour, and rising from the Moon's surface. It had to have been engineered and constructed at some point after the impact, by an alien civilisation. It was the only conclusion that could be drawn from the surreal sight in front of them.

"My God! We appear to be looking at some kind of alien structure, built within the impact crater. It seems to have risen from below the Moon's surface judging by the small ridge of crater ejecta surrounding the object. My guess is that it's some kind of transmitter, but there appears to be no radio antenna dish as such. This is just weird. We are seeing dark, revolving orb-type objects hovering around the structure. There are flat, dark panels, surrounding the object which could be capturing starlight and generating power. The entire thing is surrounded by a halo of brilliant, blue light, coming from...wait—" Scott reported what they were seeing back to Groom Lake Mission Control above the heavy interference.

The blue light was now strengthening and had formed into an intense glowing orb about the size of a football. The astronauts watched as the orb started moving around the edge of the base of the crater, before slowing again. It hovered momentarily, and then started moving up the bank towards them.

"Move… Move!" was all Scott could shout, as the blue orb started accelerating up the crater towards them.

Bannister felt an immense heat, and then images; moving images like a movie being played quickly over in his mind. He felt love, anger, power, humility, and fear. Finally, he saw an image of the object they were both looking at actually being constructed, and then he finally understood why. *No, please no, it couldn't be. We deserve another chance!*

The blue light intensified, and then, in a flash of searing pain, everything went black.

CHAPTER 27

ARMSTRONG FINALLY MANAGED to release the safety catch on the M14 and promptly let off a three-round burst of 7.62×51mm NATO cartridges, which tore into the creature's chest, forcing it backwards and down onto the ground, where it lay, whimpering in deep, guttural tones.

The sounds reminded Tom of the attack at the campsite and a shiver shot up his spine in response. "Jesus, that was close," Armstrong said, wiping perspiration from his brow.

"What in the hell is going on here? Where did that thing just come from? Was that dark void some kind of portal from another time zone, or even another planet?" Bruce asked, nonplussed at what he'd just witnessed.

Tom shook his head, trying to piece together what he'd just seen. It did kind of make sense. The mystery harpoon devices, clearly looked as if they were from another planet, or perhaps from Earth's distant future, or more worryingly, alien in origin. Could they all have just witnessed a wormhole opening up; a theoretical passage through space-time that allowed shortcuts across the universe? Wormholes after all, have been predicted to exist by the theory of general relativity. Such a thing could perhaps allow the creatures, Bigfoot, Yeti, whatever you wanted to call them, to come into the present from Earth's past. Tom had a bunch of questions firing off in his head, but none of them had answers, as he stared at the creature twitching on the ground.

Suddenly the alien device half-hidden within the glacier started to glow an intense blue again.

"Get down!" Tom screamed.

All five of them dived to the ground, covering their heads and fearing an explosion. They all lay on the cavern floor, bathed in indigo/blue light, the loud hum being emitted from the object vibrating around the domed cavern.

Tom lifted his midriff in surprise as his smartphone vibrated in his pocket. He reached in and grabbed it. The power bar was showing only 6% battery life left. A message had come in from his friend over at MIT.

"It's a text from Gerry," he said to the others, who were all looking at him, eyes wide with fear at what might happen next.

"Well, read it out!" Alicia shouted.

Tom brushed a film of dust from the screen, swiped it and opened the message. "Okay, here goes," he said, reading out the text.

TOM, I HOPE YOU GUYS ARE SAFE. WHAT I HAVE JUST DISCOVERED, IF CORRECT, IS INCREDIBLE AND SO DAMN SCARY I DON'T KNOW WHETHER TO TELL ANYONE, BUT FIGURED I HAVE NO CHOICE. JUST WHAT WE CAN DO ABOUT IT I DON'T KNOW...

I THOUGHT ABOUT WHAT YOU SAID ABOUT WHETHER THE SIGNAL MIGHT CONTAIN SOME KIND OF A MESSAGE, AND IF SO, HOW WE MIGHT GO ABOUT DECODING IT. WELL, I THINK YOU WERE CLOSE TO THE MARK WHEN YOU SAID ANY SIGNAL MEANT FOR US WOULD BE MADE DELIBERATELY EASY FOR US TO DECIPHER BY THE SENDER. I LOOKED AT EVERYHTING, STARTING WITH EARTH'S MOST COMMON ELEMENTS AS YOU SUGGESTED, THE PLANET'S LOCATION WITHIN THE SOLAR SYSTEM AND THE MILKY WAY ETC. BUT CAME UP WITH NOTHING. I THEN THOUGHT, WHAT IF THE MESSAGE WAS MORE GENERIC IN NATURE? WHAT IF THE SIGNAL WASN'T SPECIFICALLY MEANT FOR US, BUT WAS A MESSAGE SIMPLY CONCERNING US?

WELL, THIS IS THE SCARY PART. I TOOK THE ATOMIC NUNBERS OF THE MOST ABUNDANT GASSES IN THE UNIVERSE, HYDROGEN AND HELIUM, AND ASSIGNED THEM TO THE DECODING SOFTWARE WE'VE BEEN USING OVER HERE AND I FED IN THE SIGNAL DATA. I CANT BELIEVE THE RESULT. THE SIGNAL APPEARS TO BE USING A FAIRLY SIMPLE MEANS OF COMMUNICATION. IT'S PURE MATHS AND EASY FOR ANY ADVANCED CIVILIZATION TO DECODE, BUT HERE'S THE SCARY PART. THIS APPEARS TO BE THE TRANSLATION;

586743-3953974397 48 (REPRESSENTS OUR SUN'S POSITION WITHIN THE MILKY WAY GALAXY) THEN 3 (EARTH IS THE THIRD PLANET FROM THE SUN) AND THEN THIS – SPECIES: HOMO SAPIEN... NUMBERS... POPULATION GROWTH... WARS... DEATH... FAMINE, POLAR REGIONS MELTING... SPECIES EXTINCTION... TECHNOLOGY, NUCLEAR FISSION/FUSION... UNVIABLE... TERMINATION.

THE SIGNAL DOESN'T APPEAR TO BE FOR US, BUT IS ABOUT US. I BELIEVE THE SIGNAL IS ALERTING OTHER ADVANCED CIVILIZATIONS NEARBY THAT WE ARE ABOUT TO BE TERMINATED. SOMEONE HAS DECIDED WE POSE TOO MUCH RISK TO THE SOLAR SYSTEM, PERHAPS THE GALAXY. TOM, IN SHORT, I BELIEVE WE'RE ALL SCREWED!

"That's it. That's all it says," Tom said, shielding his eyes from the blue glow coming from the object, his mind spinning.

"Is he being freaking serious?" Alicia replied.

"Well, it doesn't sound like a bloody joke to me!" Jessica added, mascara streaked under her eyes from where she'd been crying.

"Hold on, I have an idea. I have to text him back, but my bloody battery is about to die," Tom said, frantically typing out a message.

GERRY. I HAVE THE MESSAGE. WE ARE IN THE CAVERN AND THERE IS A DEVICE HERE. IT MUST BE THE TRANSMITTER, AND SOME KIND OF TIME TRAVEL/WORMHOLE TECHNOLOGY COMBINED. WE WITNESSED A WORMHOLE OR SOME KIND OF TIME PORTAL/GATE OPENING UP, PERHAPS TO ANOTHER DIMENSION OR ANOTHER WORLD. I HAVE AN IDEA. WE NEED TO TRY TO TRANSMIT SOMETHING BACK. GERRY, FEED THIS INTO THE TRANSLATION SOFTWARE AND SEND ME THE AUDIO OF THE TRANSLATED TEXT BACK. DO IT NOW!

*THIS IS A MESSAGE FROM PLANET EARTH - 586743-3953974397 48 – 3. PLEASE GIVE US ANOTHER CHANCE. WE CHERISH OUR PLANET AND ALL THE LIFEFORMS ON IT. AS A SPECIES, WE ARE CAPABLE OF SUCH BEAUTIFUL DREAMS, AND SUCH HORRIBLE NIGHTMARES. WE WILL DESTROY YOUR MACHINE, BUT DO NOT TAKE THIS AS AN ACT OF AGGRESSION. WE SEEK PEACE AND FRIENDSHIP. WE ARE ALL BORN FROM THE STARS... I SEND ON THE FOLLOWING COMMENT, WHICH IS FROM ONE OF EARTH'S GREATEST INHABITANTS, THE PHYSICIST, CARL SAGAN – **"THE NITROGEN IN OUR DNA, THE CALCIUM IN OUR TEETH, THE IRON IN OUR BLOOD, THE CARBON IN OUR APPLE PIES WERE MADE IN THE INTERIORS OF COLLAPSING STARS. WE ARE MADE OF STARSTUFF."***

Tom read his message out to the others. "It's all I can think of saying," he said, once he'd finished.

"Nice quote, but what the hell? Do you seriously think you can communicate with aliens?" Alicia asked.

"It's ridiculous, Tom, but it might be our only chance. I hope you're filming all this, Bruce," Armstrong added.

"Damn right," Bruce replied, propped up on his elbows and lying on his belly a short distance away. "The battery will die soon though."

Tom hit the send button.

Almost immediately, another text came through from Gerry.

NOT GOOD NEWS. THE ODYSSEY MISSION APPEARS TO HAVE GONE WRONG. ALL CONTACT HAS BEEN LOST WITH THE ASTRONAUTS AND THE WHITEHOUSE HAS ORDERED A DIRECT STRIKE ON COBALT RIDGE GLACIER. I'M SORRY, MY FRIEND, BUT IT LOOKS AS IF THIS THING IS NOW OUT OF CONTROL. GOD HELP YOU ALL.

Tom's stomach flipped over in fear and panic as he read the message. *No, this can't be the end!* He bit his lip and stopped himself from immediately reading the message out to the others, but they had a right to know what was about to happen.

He checked the battery life on his phone. Only 2% remained. *"Shit... shit. Come on, Gerry, send me the audio file!"* he screamed.

The blue light in the cavern was getting more intense, and the electrical hum louder as the device appeared to be powering up for some kind of an event. Tom feared that another wormhole or portal was about to open up. "Gerry, sent me a text. It's not good news. The Whitehouse have ordered a direct strike against this location. If you want to leave the cavern, now is your chance. I have to wait here for Gerry's audio file," Tom said, just as the power indicator on his smartphone dropped to 1%.

"Those fucking idiots! What are they doing?" Alicia screamed. "Screw them, we're staying here with you, Tom."

"I'm so sorry, Jess. I didn't mean things to end like this," Tom said, squeezing her hand.

"It's okay babe. You were right. We had to come back up here for Maddy and Conner," she said, wiping away a tear.

"Come on, Gerry, send us that god-damned audio file!" Armstrong shouted, refusing to resign to his fate.

The five of them waited, bathed in blue light as they lay on the cavern floor, heads close together and staring at the smartphone gripped in Tom's trembling hand.

CHAPTER 28

Mount Shasta, 3 A.M.

"WHAT THE HELL do you mean they're going to obliterate the site?" Dr Lucy Davies shouted angrily at Lieutenant Jordan, who'd just come off his sat-phone.

"I'm afraid its game over. We have no choice, the Moon mission has failed. All contact with the astronauts has been lost. We can only fear the worst. The president has ordered a strike against the glacier and the device or transmitter, whatever is buried down there. We are expendable. A squadron of F-35s are en route now from Beale. You are free to leave if you wish, but I don't think you'll get very far. It's been a pleasure to have worked with you," Jordan said bluntly, raising his right hand in a salute.

"Fuck you! Come on, Fred; let's get the hell out of here, *NOW!*" Lucy screamed, as the distant roar of jet engines could be heard from somewhere lower down in the valley.

Lucy and Professor Beck started to sprint along the ridge towards where the SETI truck was parked up. They were thirty feet away from the vehicle when Lucy suddenly slipped on the ice and fell to the frozen ground, screaming as she did.

Running alongside her, Professor Beck turned as he heard her scream, seeing Lucy on her stomach, sliding towards the edge of the ridge, and a forty-foot steep drop-off to the forest below.

Beck ran back a few paces and stooped down, reaching out to grab Lucy's hand. As he did, there was a roar from overhead as a squadron of six F-35 stealth jets flew low over the ridge, kicking up snow and ice and whipping the tops of the fir trees below them.

"This is Squadron Leader Colonel Gus Mitchell – Albatross. We have reached the site. Military personnel and civilians are on the ground. I repeat, military personnel and civilians on the ground. The site appears secure. Confirm strike instructions. I repeat confirm strike," he said, speaking into his helmet mic, as he banked the 5th generation F-35 Lightning II fighter jet away from the mountain.

The six aircraft flew low over the trees in a wide loop, as Mitchell awaited orders from Beale. As he did, he monitored the information being projected on to his Helmet Mounted Display System, which gave him data on airspeed, heading, altitude, targeting information, and warnings. It was the red warning text that had just lit up in the middle of the screen that he wasn't expecting to see. Never in any of his operational training had he received confirmation that the advanced craft was being tracked by some kind of enemy radar system. He immediately hit the afterburners and accelerated at a near vertical climb, the aircraft rapidly accelerating to Mach 1, five seconds later. The other five aircraft followed.

The warning text on the HMDS blinked out as Mitchell reached an altitude of nineteen thousand feet.

"This is Beale Strike Command. Mission is a go. I repeat, mission is a go. Strike… Strike… Strike," came the order.

Mitchell banked the F-35 right. As he did, the jet's Distributed Aperture System—DAS, gave him 360-degree, high resolution real-time display from six infrared cameras mounted around the aircraft of the eastern flank of Mount Shasta and the Cobalt Ridge Glacier below.

The F-35 used Electro-Optical Targeting System—EOTS, the world's first and only sensor that combined forward-looking infrared—FLIR, and infrared search and track—IRST functionality, allowing Mitchell to fire the jet's precision air-to-surface missiles with pin-point accuracy towards the target embedded in the glacier. Less than a second later, the four missiles streaked towards the ridge below.

The roar from the F-35 jets took Professor Beck by surprise, causing him to slip and misjudge Lucy's open hand, letting Lucy slip out of reach, off the ridge, and down the forty-foot drop of towards the tree line below.

As she fell, her view was of the deep blue sky and the four white contrails from the missiles now bearing down at the ridge from above. "Run, save yourself professor," she screamed, as she slipped down the steep bank. The last thing she saw before blacking out was a wall of brilliant, blue light, fanning out from high up in the sky like a beautiful, blue shimmering waterfall, which seemed to envelop the entire mountain.

Mitchell tracked the missiles from twenty-thousand feet as they streaked towards their target below. He whispered a prayer for his colleagues, and the civilians still on the ground. But then, to his utter disbelief, he watched as a spherical orb of blue light appeared from nowhere below, two thousand feet above the ridge. The light then fanned out in a blink of an eye, forming a transparent blue dome above the site and the side of the mountain. He observed the missiles as they struck the blue aura, exploding on impact. His first thought, despite the absurdity, was that it was some kind of force field.

"Missiles have failed to hit target, I repeat failed to hit target. Launching a second wave," Mitchell reported.

The pilot gave the orders to his squadron to each launch two more air-to-surface missiles at the target. The five F-35 pilots complied with the directive and seconds later, another ten

ASM's blasted from the jets underbelly and streaked down towards Cobalt Ridge below.

Colonel Mitchell's EOTS system kept track of the missiles as they sped towards their target; ten thousand feet...eight thousand feet...six thousand feet. Suddenly, way below, the faint blue haze that had appeared earlier became more intense, and then ten bright flashes, split seconds apart, expanded into hundred-foot diameter explosions from the spent missiles, which fanned out over the curved dome of blue above the ridge.

"Albatross to base. We have a mission failure. We are dealing with an unknown technology that appears to have created some kind of force-field over the target. I repeat..." Mitchell hesitated. "Shit, we're being tracked again. I have enemy radar lock-on. Stealth appears inoperative. Taking evasive action," Mitchell shouted, pushing the throttle stick on his F-35 fully forward and accelerating to Mach 1.8 in a large arc over the Shasta Trinity National Park.

The other five jets followed, but it was too late.

"Incoming!" Mitchell screamed into his helmet as six streaks of blue light erupted from the hazy blue dome below and raced towards the jets at ten times the speed of sound. Less than a split second later, the jets vanished in flashes of tiny blue particles, leaving just empty sky, white contrails and silence.

CHAPTER 29

MULTIPLE EXPLOSIONS ECHOED along the mineshaft, sending a small blast wave that rocked the cavern, causing the ground to rumble, and loose pieces of rock and quartz to fall from the walls and roof of the cave

"Jesus what just happened?" Armstrong asked.

"I don't know, but it wasn't the volcano. It sounded like an over ground explosion. Maybe they are trying to blast their way into the cavern from above," Tom said, still gripping and staring at his smartphone.

Buzz... buzz, the phone suddenly vibrated in his hand. "It's a message; the audio file!" he shouted, quickly opening up the message. Sure enough, Gerry had managed to send him an audio file attachment, timed at 03.12. There was no time to think or even listen to it, the phone's battery was about to die on him.

He rushed over to the alien device protruding from the exposed section of melting glacier ice above, which had penetrated the far corner of the cavern's ceiling. The weird black material the device was made from was like nothing he'd ever seen before. It was black, yet translucent in places, allowing for brief flashes of the rock and ice behind it, as if the dark material were continuously moving inside the object, almost as if it were alive.

Tom reached out and touched the device. He could feel a deep, pulsating *hum* coming from it. He felt warmth and then cold and could see the colours of the rainbow, prisms of light in his mind as he ran his hand over it. He brushed away a thin layer of ice crystals, hit the play button on his phone, and placed it flat against the object. He could hear the audio file, almost like whale-song in some parts, mixed with static, white noise, and a high-pitched squeaking sound that you used to hear when downloading a game onto a computer via a cassette tape in the 1980s. Then Tom heard the two beeps that confirmed the battery on his phone had finally died.

He pulled the smartphone away from the object, and checked. The screen was black, but he'd heard the audio, it had played out. If the device could somehow absorb the sound, the message may well be on its way to whoever had sent the coded signal–or so he hoped.

Tom turned to the others, his back to the object. "Well, the audio file has been sent. I think it's finally time to get the hell out of here before this cave collapses." As he spoke Alicia and Jessica screamed.

"Mate, just bloody run and don't look back!" Armstrong shouted, as he stood and squeezed the trigger on the M14, letting off a series of three-round bursts, the sound exploding in the confines of the small cavern.

An instant surge of adrenalin rushed into Tom's veins in response to the fear he suddenly felt and he sprinted across the fifteen feet to the small gap where they'd entered the cavern. The other four were also scrambling to their feet, and from the look on the girl's faces, something was seriously spooking them.

Tom reached the cavern wall and turned back towards the device. The cavern was now filled with an indigo light, not from the device, but from the harpoon-like objects stacked up beneath the device or transmitter, whatever the thing was. A blue haze had also now formed, and an even larger black eye had opened up in the middle of the haze. About to come through the void, and shrouded in a white, misty substance, were what appeared to be a number of silver-suited, humanoid-shaped entities.

Tom glanced at his backpack, which was still on the floor, the harpoon-like tool still sticking out the back, and now also glowing brightly, and he dived onto it, pulling the device free. It immediately welded itself to his hand again, as if it had been designed for only him to hold. His only thought was of fear and of destroying the device and black void in front of him. As he thought about it, a questioned popped into his mind.

Are you certain you want to take this action?

Tom answered the question with a thought—*yes*.

As he did, a thin line of blue light, like a laser beam, shot out from the end of the harpoon and struck the transmitter, enveloping the ice-buried device, and causing it to spark, as if it were short circuiting. The blue aura it had been emitting suddenly faded, and the black eye vanished with a pop of static as quickly as it had appeared. As it blinked out, one of the entities appeared to make an effort to push through the vanishing void into the cavern, but was unable to make it. As the black eye disappeared, a severed forelimb, or arm, still encased in its silver spacesuit, landed on the cave floor.

Before any of them could speak, the humming sound coming from the device started to get louder, and the device began to change colour from black, to indigo-blue and then to a burnt orange.

"Run! I think it's going to explode!" Tom screamed.

The five of them dived for the narrow opening towards the mineshaft and squeezed through into the tunnel beyond. Safely through, they sprinted along the tunnel, the intense light from the cavern illuminating their way in an eerie band of colours. They ran over the bone field, reached the intersection in the tunnel, and turned left into the long passage that led to the mine's entrance and the clearing where they'd set up camp. As they ran, a massive explosion erupted from the cavern behind them.

"Move... Move!" Tom urged, stealing a quick glance behind him and seeing a huge fireball advancing along the tunnel towards the intersection.

The five of them managed to run another thirty feet along the tunnel before being hit by a massive blast wave from the explosion.

Tom was thrown forward through the air by the force and smashed against one of the tunnel's wooden, support beams. His head spun momentarily, before everything went black.

CHAPTER 30

TOM'S HEAD WAS pounding, as if he'd just woken with one of the worst hangovers of his life. As he opened his eyes his vision blurred, and all he could see was a white haze. A rhythmical *beep... beep... beep* becoming apparent from over on his left, and a chill raced up his spine as the events in the cavern slowly came back to him. *What had happened? Were they still in the mine?*

He sat bolt upright, his head spinning with confusion. As his vision slowly returned to normal and he took in his surroundings a wave of panic descended over him. *Had he been abducted?*

He was wired up to the machine that was beeping away; clear tubes stretched from a cannula fitted into his left arm and were wired up to the device that was next to the bed he was lying in.

The room was all white, clinical. As he thought about where he might be, the machine by his bed started beeping rapidly as he began to panic, causing adrenalin to flood into his veins. *Flight or fight?* was his only thought.

He fell back into the bed, and reached over to pull out the tube from the cannula protruding from his arm. Just as he did, he heard a voice.

"Don't even think about doing that, Mr. Bishop," a stern female voice shouted.

Tom cricked his neck as he whipped his head around to see who had spoken, sending a burning spasm through his neck and shoulder.

A woman, wearing a blue nurse's uniform rushed over to the side of Tom's bed and quickly inserted the tube back into the back of his hand. "Tut… tut… tut, now that was a very silly thing to do. You're receiving saline and antibiotics for a nasty gash to your head and thigh. There's no knowing what sort of bugs are lurking in that old copper mine they found you in," she said, in a calm but authoritative voice.

"Jeez, where am I?" Tom asked.

"You're in the Shasta Mount View City Hospital. A search party brought you in. They found you all in the mineshaft after the landslide on the mountain. Luckily for you, the old mines didn't collapse. They must have been constructed well. You guys were all lucky."

Tom closed his eyes. His head started to spin again, his memory of the events hazy.

"Where are my friends?"

"Don't you worry about them, they will be okay. One of the chaps has had to have an emergency operation on his arm though. He's lost it unfortunately, but he'll be okay. He's recovering now in intensive care. Your other three friends were released yesterday. You've been in a medically induced coma for three days, but don't worry, you're on the mend, and your family have been informed. Dr Holland will be around to check on you in an hour or so. Can I get you something to drink in the meantime?"

Tom felt dizzy as he tried to think about everything that had happened. "Yes, please, a cup of tea would be good."

"I'll sort that out for you," the nurse smiled at him as she headed for the door. "Don't you dare try to pull that tube out again now will you."

"Sorry, I was a little scared and not thinking straight when I woke up. Oh do you know where my phone is? I'd like to contact my family if possible."

"Of course. You're not supposed to use it in here, but I'll fetch it for you. Sometimes rules are meant to be broken, eh!" The nurse winked and left the room.

She returned twenty minutes later with a cup of tea and his smartphone, which had been fully charged.

"This should help," she said, putting the cup of tea down on the table by his bed. "Make sure you're not on that thing when Dr Holland comes in to see you," she said, as she turned and left the room.

Tom grabbed his phone and opened the text messages that were waiting for him. There were two missed calls from his mother and also a text message. Naturally, she and his father were worried sick about him and had wanted to fly over, but the hospital had advised against it. They had been informed that Tom had been given a CT scan and was fine.

The next message was from Jessica, confirming she'd been discharged, and that she was okay and on her way home. She'd been told he had been put into a medically induced coma but that he was okay. She wanted him to contact her as soon as he woke and hoped he could stop by and stay at her parents' house for a few nights once he was out of hospital.

That sounds like a great idea right now, Tom thought.

The third message was from his friend Gerry over at MIT.

DID YOU GET THE AUDIO FILE? I MANAGED TO CONVERT THE MESSAGE USING THE TRANSLATION SOFTWARE. NO IDEA IF IT WILL WORK THOUGH. TXT TO CONFIRM YOU MANAGED TO SOMEHOW UPLOAD IT. GERRY.

There was a second message.

JESUS, TOM, WHAT'S HAPPENED? NO WORD FROM YOU NOW FOR TWENTY-FOUR HOURS. I'M WORRIED SICK. I FOUND OUT FROM U.S. MILITARY E-MAIL INTERCEPTS THAT SIX F-35'S VANISHED OVER COBALT RIDGE AROUND THE TIME YOU GUYS WERE IN THE CAVERN. ARMY PERSONNEL AND THE SETI CREW ON THE GROUND AT THE TIME ARE ALL SAFE. THERE'S BEEN NO WORD AS TO WHAT HAPPENED ON THE MOON AND DESPITE MY BEST EFFORTS TO HACK BACK INTO THE NASA

SITE I'VE FOUND NOTHING. THE OFFICIAL STORY THAT'S BEING DISSEMINATED IS THAT A LANDSLIDE FOLLOWING A SMALL ERUPTION OF MOUNT SHASTA BURIED COBALT RIDGE IN FIVE FEET OF SNOW AND ROCK AND THAT A SEARCH AND RESCUE PARTY HAS BEEN SENT OUT.

Tom scrolled to the third and final message from Gerry and quickly opened it.

THANK GOD. I'VE JUST MANAGED TO TRACK YOU GUYS TO THE MOUNT VIEW HOSPITAL. BEEN TOLD YOU'RE OK BUT IN AN INDUCED COMA. JESUS, TOM, IT MUST HAVE BEEN CRAZY UP ON THE MOUNTAIN. I CAN'T WAIT FOR YOU TO FILL ME IN ON EVERYTHING THAT HAPPENED.
ONE LAST THING – THERE'S GOING TO BE AN EMERGENCY NASA/ US GOVERNMENT DEBRIEF ENQUIRY AND THEY'RE GOING TO CALL THE BOTH OF US TO GIVE EVIDENCE. SEEMS OUR TEXT MESSAGES WERE INTERCEPTED. ANYWAY, YOU GET BETTER AND I'LL SEE YOU SOON FOR A BEER, MATE.

Jesus, a NASA/U.S. Government debrief? That will be interesting, Tom thought, reaching over for his tea. He gulped it down, the warm drink spreading through his abdomen. It felt good.

Suddenly, the door opened and a tall, slim, grey-haired man wearing a suit, walked in. "Good morning, Tom, I'm Dr Holland," he said, holding out his hand for Tom to shake. "Nurse Alexandra told me you had come around. Just lie back, please, I need to examine you."

Tom did as instructed, and Dr Holland placed the stethoscope at various points on his chest and carried out a blood pressure test. "We had to put you into an induced coma due to your head injury. Thankfully, the scans showed no evidence of a bleed to the brain. You were very lucky."

"I guess."

Dr Holland looked at him. "Unfortunately, I'm not permitted to discuss any of the events that led to you being here, but from what I've heard on the news, they sound very intriguing."

There was a moment's silence. "Hmm, yes, you could say that Doctor. I'm feeling a little confused right now to be honest."

"I'm sure."

As he spoke, there was a knock on the door and another man appeared, wearing a dark suit and looking more official. He beckoned Dr Holland over.

Dr Holland stood and spoke briefly with the man. Tom heard his name being mentioned, before Dr Holland headed back over, a serious look on his face.

"Okay, things are moving quicker than I thought. I've been advised that a helicopter will be coming to pick you up at four p.m., five hours from now. You'd better have a rest. I'll check you once more before you leave," Dr Holland said, then quickly left the room.

Tom felt his head spinning again and flopped back down onto his pillow, closed his sore eyes, and felt himself quickly drift back to sleep.

CHAPTER 31

THE ROTORS OF the Apache attack helicopter produced a rhythmical *thump… thump… thump* as the craft banked slowly over the town of Shasta and the edge of the Shasta Trinity National Park, before the nose dropped and the twin turboshafts accelerated the chopper towards the southwest, where Tom had been told a small, government scientific team, with the highest level of security clearance, were waiting to see him.

He'd been woken up in the hospital after his brief sleep and given a final check, as promised by Dr Holland, who'd authorised his discharge, on the basis that he must take things easy for the next forty-eight hours.

After ninety minutes the Apache started to slow and banked left before quickly descending. Tom looked out the window, but there wasn't a lot to see. Woodland stretched out on one side, farmland on the other. Wherever they were, it was a fair way from any densely populated urban area.

The chopper landed on a makeshift helipad in a large field and the rotors immediately started powering down. Within a few minutes, Tom was ushered out of the Apache by the pilot and over to a black 4x4 with the blue and white SETI logo on the side that was waiting a short distance away. The fact that he was meeting with scientists from SETI eased his tension slightly as he thought at least they should be sympathetic to his actions.

The 4x4 was fitted out with darkened glass, a black leather interior and a central console, filled with an assortment of bottled water, Coke, and some glasses. Fitted to the divider screen between the front cabin and rear section, was a flat monitor, which was showing what looked like a SETI promotional video. Images of rolling farmland, a wooden barn, what looked like a high-tech SETI training centre, and a small array of deep-space radio antennae dishes, together with a vast bank of solar panels that stretched for acres across one of the adjacent fields was being shown.

The 4x4 drove onto a rural track and headed towards what appeared to be a large, wooden farmhouse about half a mile from the helipad, and pulled up into the courtyard. The driver killed the engine, jumped out, and opened the rear door for Tom. "Just head over there, sir," he said pointing. "It's the main entrance. Someone will be there to greet you. I'll be waiting here to take you back to the helipad."

Tom did as he was instructed and was greeted by an auburn-haired female, wearing glasses, and dressed formally in a dark jacket and trousers. "Good evening, Mr. Bishop. Follow me, please," she said.

Tom followed the woman along an ultra-modern looking corridor, lit from above by inset, bright strip lighting, which looked totally alien compared with the external appearance of the wooden-structured building. The fake farmhouse was clearly just rural camouflage for the high-tech building it disguised. The walls of the corridor were smooth, white, and adorned with framed photographs of NASA astronauts, and beautiful images of the Milky Way Galaxy captured by the Hubble Space Telescope.

The woman stopped by a door with black Perspex plaque on it with white lettering - Meeting Room 1.

She knocked on the door and opened it. "Please, go in and take a seat."

Tom nodded and walked into the white-walled, sterile meeting room where five individuals were seated behind a long, white table at the rear of the room, four men and an attractive, dark-haired woman. Seated on a small, central round table was his best friend Gerry, dressed casually in a blue shirt and jeans. A large, black monitor took up most of the space on one of the four walls.

Gerry gave Tom a broad smile as he entered. Tom was glad to see him, and he grinned back, and nodded to his good friend and colleague.

The female stood as Tom entered the room. "Good evening, Mr. Bishop. I'm Dr Lucy Davies. These are my colleagues Professor Fred Beck, and Dr Hans Willems. We are all SETI scientists based over at Mountain View in California. The two gentlemen to my right are Major Joseph Grant from the U.S. Army and Dr Edgar Bond from NASA. We're very sorry to have whisked you straight over here into this formal setting from your hospital bed. We're are fully aware of what you've been through, but I'm sure you can imagine we needed to speak with you as soon as we could, as there are a number of question we would like answers to, if you have any, in light of the... well the extraordinary series of events that have taken place over the last ten days."

Tom took a seat next to his friend. "No problem, Dr Davies. I'm feeling a little tired, but Dr Holland seems to have looked after me well," he said, touching the bandage that covered the nasty gash to the right side of his temple.

"That's good, and please, you can call me Lucy. Help yourself to a drink. There's water, tea, and coffee over on the side."

Tom saw that Gerry already had a glass of water, so he got up and poured himself a mug of coffee, before sitting back down.

"So, Tom, we just need you to firstly take us through your background a little, your knowledge of the work SETI does and the reason for you being on Mount Shasta on the weekend of September sixteen last," Lucy said.

"Sure," Tom said, starting by telling them why he and his three friends had gone to the mountain in the first place. The camping trip had been nothing more than an end of summer fun weekend for them all, before his heavy schedule working on the exo-solar planet research he was involved in as part of his Masters over at MIT started again. Tom explained that he was originally from Cardiff, a city in Wales, U.K. He had been drawn to the exciting research in his chosen field of study being carried out at MIT. He then took them through the events that had occurred on the first night, which had led him and Jessica walking into the gun store owned by Casey and his son, and their subsequent return to the mountain to look for their friends and help make a documentary being filmed by Casey's friend, the U.K. documentary filmmaker, Richard Armstrong.

The NASA scientist, Dr Bond, then asked him a question. "Can I ask you about the creature that you say attacked you at the campsite? The creature I understand that was also responsible for lassoing two of Mr. Armstrong's cameramen and dragging them to their deaths in the forest, not to mention the loss of one of the U.S. Military's Humvees, and I understand the killing of a bear in the forest during which the unfortunate animal had one of its forelimbs ripped off. I mean, do you have any theory on this? Are saying you witnessed a Bigfoot attack up on the mountain, Mr Bishop?"

Tom cleared his throat. "It sounds extraordinary I know, but we all saw what you just described. The creatures are real, but I believe they come from Earth's distant past and were somehow able to travel to the present using the device entrapped in the thawing glacier.

General Grant looked at Tom. "You're suggesting the Bigfoot was able to use the device to time travel?" he asked, smirking slightly.

"I don't know, sir. It's just a theory," Tom replied.

"So, this harpoon weapon you refer to. Do you think there is any chance there could be more of them lying around the Trinity National Park?" The general asked.

Tom shrugged. "It's possible for sure, but we didn't see any others."

"On the same note, I don't suppose you can help with what may have happened to our F-35's?"

"No, sorry," Tom said, shrugging his shoulders again.

The general made a note on a pad he had in front of him and looked over at Lucy and Professor Beck.

Lucy nodded and then looked at Tom. "Your friend, Gerry, has kindly told us about how he went about deciphering the alien signal. Although we don't condone his actions, we are, of course, hugely impressed by how he achieved this. We are even more impressed by the message you asked him to translate back using the helium/nitrogen atomic number code. What we wish to know is if you managed to transmit that message before the events that led to you being in hospital?"

Tom slowly nodded, fearing he was about to be arrested for breaching some kind of UN/government protocol on the transmission of signals to alien civilizations. "Well, I didn't do anything very technical. I simply placed my phone up against the object and played the audio file. The audio message played out just before my phone's battery died. I'm figuring that the message got back to Cassiopeia though."

"Oh, and what makes you think that, Mr. Bishop?" Dr Edgar Bond asked.

"It's just a hunch. A feeling I had as I pressed the phone against the object."

"I see."

Dr Lucy Davies continued her questioning. "The text from Gerry to yourself which refers to Earth's population, wars etc., Can you give us your theory on what this means?"

Tom took in a deep breath. He knew this question was going to be asked and he had been mulling over the answer since he'd read Gerry's message. "Well, I've thought a lot about it and the answer I have come to isn't very reassuring, I'm afraid. My theory is that whoever sent the signal was transmitting a kind of *failed planet* notice out to any civilization technologically advanced enough to decipher the message. I believe the coded signal was an alert, confirming the human species have effectively screwed everything up and it's time to eliminate the threat we and Planet Earth might bring to the solar system, or this region of space if anything catastrophic were to happen. Let's face it, despite what most politicians say, most climate scientists know the planet is heating up from runaway global warming, Earth's population is expanding at an exponential rate, and the natural resources vital to our survival are running out faster than we can replace them with sustainable alternatives. I guess our neighbours have had enough and are thinking; why wait for us to wipe ourselves out by nuclear extinction when they can do things more effectively and safer themselves?"

The panel in front looked at him in silence, before General Grant replied. "Those are very serious and profound comments, Tom."

Tom shrugged. "You asked my opinion. That's it."

"I think we have come as far as we can with this. We need to wrap things up here. You are free to leave. As you might expect, what happened on the mountain must remain out of the public domain, and all personnel on the mountain, including you and your friends have been sworn to secrecy. Needless to say, prosecution will follow if this protocol is not followed," The NASA official said.

Tom stood to leave.

"Oh, there's one last thing. Do you have any proof, or evidence for anything you've told us, Tom?" General Grant asked.

"Well, yes, Armstrong's cameraman captured the entire event on video. There's plenty of proof."

General Grant sighed and shrugged. "Unfortunately, the footage was blank. We've examined the camera," he said, with a wry smile.

"Well, I guess that means you'll find your F-35's soon then," Tom said, sarcastically.

The general gave a forced smile. "Touché"

Lucy cleared her throat to break the ice and smiled. "Thank you both for coming today, our discussion has been very helpful. I'll see you out," she said, standing up.

Lucy walked them both back along the corridor. "The driver who brought you here has been instructed to drive you wherever you want to go, within the state. Or you can be driven back to the helicopter and dropped at the nearest airport. It's up to you."

"Where are we, by the way?" Tom asked.

"Oregon," Lucy replied, with a smile.

As they reached the main door, Lucy handed them a business card each. "Listen, I'm hugely impressed with what you guys did, so are my SETI colleagues. It was the right thing in the circumstances. Please give me a call. There are jobs waiting for you both at SETI should you want them. We're going to be very busy and we need guys like you working with us."

"Thanks. I'm sure we'll give it some serious thought," Tom said, smiling back.

The pair of them walked out into the yard. The wind was whipping up loose hay and blowing it over from the adjoining fields where Tom had noticed a number of bales stacked up against the perimeter hedge-row. They walked over to the black 4X4 waiting a short distance away.

"Where are we heading gentlemen?" The driver asked.

Tom looked at his friend. "Can you recommend a good bar? We both need a good chat over some beers and good food."

The driver nodded and winked. "Not a problem. I know just the place. Jump in."

PROLOGUE

SEA RANCH
California, October 15

THE BILLIONS OF stars twinkled in the night sky above them. Apart from the occasional "song" from a chirping cicada, the only sound was of the waves breaking gently on the beach below the ragged cliffs a short distance away. Tom took in a deep breath of fresh air and sighed as he turned to Jessica who was lying by his side. "It's incredibly relaxing out here, and a world away from the events on Mount Shasta. I can't believe it was all only three weeks ago. It feels like a lifetime away," he said, still looking up at the night sky.

Jessica replied in a soft voice. One that he'd not heard since before they'd been attacked at the mountain campsite. "Well, I thought we could do with a proper break. Sea Ranch has always been one of my favourite spots. I just wish we'd all have come here instead of going to that damn mountain," she said, stifling a yawn.

"I can't argue with that comment," Tom said.

They were lying on a large blanket outside in the back garden of the wooden chalet they'd rented, the French doors to the lounge open behind them. The John Denver track, *Take Me Home, Country Roads,* started to play on the radio, the open doors allowing the classic melody to drift out into the garden. "I love this track."

"Hmm, talking of which, when will you be going back to the U.K.?" Jessica asked.

"Well, I promised my folks I'd go and see them as soon as we'd spent some time together, so, in a week or two I guess. But I won't be gone for long," he said, leaning over to kiss her on the lips.

"You'd better not!"

Before Tom could respond, his phone, which was on the blanket next to him, vibrated.

"Hello, who's that?" he said, picking up the phone and looking at the screen. He swiped the screen to open the message. The sender's details were blank. The screen then lit up with a string of numbers, too many to count. As Tom tried to take a screen shot of the odd message, the phone went blank and the text message vanished as quickly as it had appeared.

"Bloody weird," Jessica said.

Tom suddenly realised what it might be and looked back up at the canvas of stars in the heavens, quickly locating the constellation of Cassiopeia. It was one of forty-eight constellations listed by the 2nd-century Greek astronomer, Ptolemy. Tom could easily recognise it due to its distinctive "W" shape, formed by the five bright stars Alpha, Beta, Gamma, Delta, and Epsilon Cassiopeia located opposite the Big Dipper.

He stared at the approximate location of HR 8832, a main sequence star approximately 21.25 light years from Earth and wondered what the hell the sender of the signal SETI had picked up thought of his response. *Perhaps they'd been surprised, impressed even that the inhabitants of Planet Earth had managed to decode the message. Not only that, but respond to it? Had they postponed sending what had clearly been some kind of advanced invasion party maybe? Had they decided to give us one last chance?*

He didn't have any of the answers, apart from the fact that he now knew humankind was not alone in the universe, and this knowledge alone was both scary and comforting at the same time. He hoped that the powers that be would take what had happened as a stark warning to look after the planet and all of its amazing creatures. Earth, after all, is the only home we all have in the vast and incredible universe.

THE END

The author's next book – Robert Spire Action Thriller 5 – will be out, late 2018.

Please continue reading for a sample of TIPPING POINT, and links to the author's other books.

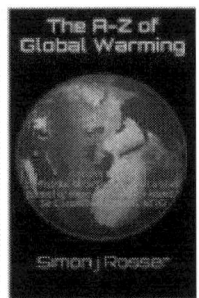

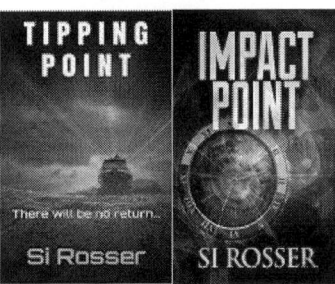

Author Bio

Simon Rosser LIb, was born in Cardiff, South Wales, UK, in 1968. He is a personal injury lawyer and author of Action-Adventure-thriller and Sci-Fi novels with an Ecological/Apocalyptic theme.

Favorite authors: Ed McBain, James Patterson, Lee Child, Lincoln Child, Douglas Preston, Patrick Lee, Clive Cussler, A.G Riddle and Michael Grumley.

Favorite movies: Good The Bad and The Ugly, Jaws, Deliverance, Star Wars, Close Encounters of the Third Kind, It's A Wonderful Life, Scarface, Play Misty For Me, Electra-Glide In Blue, The Abyss and many others.

Books - THE A-Z OF GLOBAL WARMING, Climate Fiction eco-thriller; TIPPING POINT (Robert Spire 1), Techno-thriller; IMPACT POINT (Robert Spire 2), MELT ZONE (Spire 3) and CATACLYSM of the ANCIENTS (Spire 4).

The author has also written two sci-fi horror thrillers;

VAPORIZED I and II, together with espionage thriller RED MIST.

If you enjoyed reading any of my books, and have the time, please stop by and leave an Amazon review. If you scroll to the last page on your Kindle now, you will be taken to a 'review' page. All reviews are much appreciated, thanks.

Reviews help other readers decide whether to buy a book and also to find the books they want to read. So, I would be eternally grateful, once you have finished this book, if you would leave a review on Amazon, to let other potential readers know about my book. You can do this by clicking the links above or at the very end of the book.

Please visit my website www.sirosser-thriller-writer.com for further information and free e-book deals. Many thanks, for your time, Simon Rosser.

Please read on for a preview of TIPPING POINT

PROLOGUE

French Crozet Islands, April 5

"ONLY ANOTHER FOUR of these trips and we're done," Davenport shouted to his friend, as he looked back at the jagged cliffs rising out of the ocean on the bleak leeward side of the Ile de l'Est.

"Thank God! Don't ever ask me to sign up for anything like this again. After the year we've spent down here, I'm sure we'll both be exempt from having to do any further voluntary research for a while," Hawthorn replied.

Dawn was just breaking over the windswept isles, as the old wooden fishing boat chugged out of the make-shift port on Ile de l'Est, one of six islets that make up the French Crozet Islands, in the Southern Indian Ocean. The sub-Antarctic archipelago - part of the French Southern Territories since 1955 - was uninhabited, except for a small research base on the main island, Ile de la Possession.

"You know, Adam, I could think of better things to be doing during my gap year. Monitoring penguins and sea creatures doesn't feature high on the list," Hawthorn said, turning the boat towards the sampling zone.

"Don't forget it's your turn to update the catalogue; with whatever marine samples we find," Davenport shouted, throwing the well-used notebook, across the deck, to his friend.

Adam Davenport and James Hawthorn had been based on

the main island, Ile de la Possession, along with five other research scientists for the last eight months, and were now embarking on the final four months of their placement, as part of an international monitoring team, studying the many different species of penguins, seals, birds, flora and fauna unique to the archipelago. The islands were, in fact, one large nature reserve, since being declared a national park back in 1938. The two researchers felt long forgotten by the outside world. The monthly food drop, by small plane, from the French Kerguelen Islands - some 1300 kilometers to the east - was their only real comfort.

The boat's bow rose up on the crest of a wave as they motored out of the protected inlet toward Ile de la Possession, and the buoy that marked the research area, some two kilometers out from the eastern shore.

"It sure is calm out today," Davenport said, looking out over the horizon. A group of five petrels circled above the boat as they arrived at the marker buoy.

Hawthorn cut the engine, letting the boat drift toward the orange buoy. "Pass the rope, so I can tie her up," he yelled.

Davenport threw him the frayed end of the rope, which he secured to the chain on the buoy. The boat bobbed up and down on the light swell as Davenport went to retrieve his packet of Marlboro's from the wheelhouse. "How many pots are we supposed to be pulling up today, James?" he shouted over to his friend.

"Looks like we dropped eight overboard last week," Hawthorn replied, flicking through the scruffy, worn notepad which dated back to the 1960s. "It's going to look like seafood pick and mix by the time we haul them all up."

Davenport leaned over the side of the boat, taking in a deep breath of sea air. He pulled a Marlboro from the packet, licked the end of it, and placed it between his lips. "There's a very strange smell on the port side," he shouted to Hawthorn, who was getting the sampling kits ready to drop overboard.

He flipped the top of his Zippo lighter open and struck the flint. Before Hawthorn could answer him, a flash of light and heat exploded around them, completely engulfing the wooden fishing boat.

Hawthorn felt the force of the explosion as he was thrown into the shattered wheelhouse, followed by an instant of agonizing pain, then darkness.

Davenport opened his eyes. He was in the water, surrounded by flotsam, and covered in burning oil. He tried to swim through it, but the task was futile. He screamed and dived under the water. The last thing he felt was a searing pain in his lungs as he sank into the freezing depths.

CHAPTER 1

London, April 15

DR. DALE STANTON sat at his desk, in the darkening room of his Russell Square apartment, staring blankly at the glowing computer screen, his eyes tired and sore. His face was impassive, except for the visible, nervous, twitch in the corner of his mouth, which revealed his gathering thoughts.

He was putting the finishing touches to the presentation that he would be giving to the Intergovernmental Panel on Climate Change conference in Oslo, Norway, in a little under a week's time. Stanton had been working on his current project for almost eight months and the conclusions he'd reached, he had little doubt, would concern the scientific world. Reaching over, he turned on the desktop lamp and rubbed his eyes, before leaning back in his chair to stretch his aching neck.

Looking back at the monitor, he started reading over the salient parts of his presentation, to check it one final time before finishing for the evening. He resumed typing; making what he hoped was the final amendment to his paper.

We know the Ocean Thermohaline Circulation is an important Atlantic current powered by both heat (thermo) and salt content (haline) which brings warm water up from the tropics to northern latitudes. Without it, the Eastern Seaboard of the USA and climate of Northern Europe would be much colder. I have been re-analysing all the data amassed by the RAPID-WATCH program and my calculations reveal that the measuring devices have been incorrectly calibrated. Twenty-five of the thirty devices used to measure ocean flow were set by the manufacturers to measure fresh water. When calibrating the data to factor in measurements for denser salt water, the figures revealed...

Stanton jumped as the telephone on his desk rang. He took a deep breath and sighed, as he reached over his laptop to pick up the phone. "Hello!" There was no answer. "Hello!" Again, silence. He replaced the receiver. His train of thought interrupted, he sat quietly for a moment before completing the final sentence, then saved the amendments and closed the program down. He clicked on his private finance folder to check an insurance policy he knew was about to expire, and, as he did, accidentally opened the file containing a copy of his will. Perusing it, he reminded himself to amend the charitable legacies clause in order to make a gift to the team down at *RAPID. God knows, they would need all the help they could get.*

He'd had the will prepared, after receiving a large sum of money from his father, two years earlier. A colleague had recommended a local firm specialising in environmental law, with a promise that one of the firm's senior environmental lawyers, a Mr. Robert Spire, would be appointed as a co-executor. He closed the file, reminding himself to have the will amended when he returned from Oslo next week.

Stanton reached across his desk and pulled the research book he'd been using, from the shelf, to double check a couple of facts. He flicked through the pages to a section entitled *The Younger Dryas* period. Around 12,900 years ago - just as the world was slowly warming up after the last ice age - a rapid descent back to colder conditions occurred in as little as ten years or so, a mere blink of an eye, in climactic terms. A shut down of the Atlantic Ocean Thermohaline Circulation was thought to have been a possible cause of the rapid chill. Stanton's hair stood up on the back of his neck as he considered the possible ramifications of his latest research.

He closed the book, turned off his laptop, and ran his hands through his lank brown hair. He got up from his desk and looked out of his window at a deserted Russell Square and closed the blinds. He realised he'd been working for almost six hours, and it was now coming up to six P.M on Saturday evening.

He enjoyed living alone in his two-bed terraced townhouse apartment in London's Russell Square, one of only a few private residences left overlooking the park, but had noticed various businesses, as well as the University College of London, taking over most of the area during the last twenty years. The district was dotted with restaurants and bars, and in an hour he would be meeting up with an old friend for a well-earned drink in the Hotel Russo, not far from his apartment.

He briefly took hold of the memory stick containing his presentation, before putting it back down gently. The facts, figures and details of his paper were spinning around in his head. He knew he wouldn't be able to relax until he had given his talk in Oslo. He'd been over the calculations at least ten times, to ensure they were correct. He walked into the bathroom. *Unbelievable; how could they have failed to check the calibration on the measuring equipment?*

Just as he was about to get in the shower, the phone rang again. He picked up the receiver, "Hello!" There was silence on the other end. As he replaced the phone he heard a click on the line. *Not again.* He shrugged, and stepped under the shower.

Stanton was in the middle of drying himself when a text message came through from Mathew confirming the arrangements. They would be meeting in the Kings Bar at the Hotel Russo; a warm intimate wood-panelled bar, and one of Stanton's favourite local watering holes. He finished his ablutions, went to his bedroom and put on a white linen shirt, navy blue Chino trousers, socks and leather boater shoes and glanced in the mirror. He looked and felt tired. He splashed some aftershave on his face, locked the door to the apartment and headed down the hall stairs and wandered out into the warmth of a mild spring evening.

Manufactured by Amazon.ca
Bolton, ON

34747845R00102